Brave Souls

Brave Souls

Gary Porter

RESOURCE *Publications* · Eugene, Oregon

BRAVE SOULS

Resource Publications
An Imprint of Wipf and Stock Publishers
199 W. 8th Ave., Suite 3
Eugene, OR 97401

www.wipfandstock.com

PAPERBACK ISBN: 979-8-3852-0851-7
HARDCOVER ISBN: 979-8-3852-0852-4
EBOOK ISBN: 979-8-3852-0853-1
VERSION NUMBER 01/15/26

For churches & Christian families everywhere

For as the body is one and has many parts, and all the parts of that body, though many, are one body—so also is Christ. For we were all baptized by one Spirit into one body—whether Jews or Greeks, whether slaves or free—and we were all made to drink of one Spirit. So the body is not one part but many.

—1 CORINTHIANS 12:12–14

Acknowledgments

I AM SO ENORMOUSLY grateful for the opportunity to write this story. I hope I've lived up to the calling of it. It is my prayer that churches and Christian families everywhere can continue to be the hands and feet of Christ, doing God's work in this world, showing grace to one another, and bearing one other's burden—even when we disagree.

I would like, first of all, to thank my beautiful wife, my love, Krista. You continue to inspire me every single day. You are a true blessing to me. It is the great joy of my life to be your husband. I'd be a puddle.

And to my son, Noah. You are my heart and soul, the light of my life. What an incredible gift you are to us and to the world. Don't ever forget how much you are loved.

Thank you to my parents. You continue to stagger me with your love and kindness and generosity.

Thank you to my church family and to my work family at City Mission for continuing to shine the light of Christ in this dark world.

In memory of Ora Kenneth Baringer, the builder and peacemaker of our church.

Chapter 1

Saturday

She had to tell him. Today. She'd waited too long already. She told herself over and over there's nothing to be afraid of. But she knew in her heart that wasn't true. There was everything to fear. It could unravel her future and ruin the single greatest relationship of her lifetime. But she had to tell him. He deserved to know. He had to know now.

Katie Vreeland, soon to be Katie Ecchols—she didn't really like the sound of it, but she was grateful to take Dave's name and honestly relieved in some ways to leave her father's name behind—was standing in the grass beside the arch at the entrance to campus. She'd carried everything she owned out of her dorm room and dragged it across campus so she could meet Dave as soon as he pulled in under the arch. She was bursting with excitement. She hadn't seen him in over two months. Two months! She had been focused on school, trying to finish her Master's work in Counseling, and he was busy writing his thesis 300 miles away at Eastern Theological Seminary.

She realized she was smiling like an idiot as a gray minivan drove under the arch and continued on down the road to Shaeffer Hall. She must look absolutely crazy, she thought. Like some crazy happy homeless person, standing in the cold with all of her belongings scattered around her in the snow.

She looked up at the sky, dense with layers and layers of cottony, white clouds that were heavy with snow. There was one quick gray cloud that floated lower than the rest. It tumbled playfully across the sky and spun clockwise like a pinwheel. As she watched it, the quick gray cloud began to slowly pull apart like cotton candy into two distinct clouds, and they spun and danced together over the treetops. But slowly, agonizingly, they were pulling apart. The strands that were connecting them frayed thinner and thinner until they were only held together by a frail wire. The two clouds twisted in the wind held together by that frail wire for almost a full minute until finally they detached completely and hurried off in separate directions. There was something inevitable about the parting of the two gray clouds that made Katie very sad. She was powerless to stop it, and it hurt her heart somehow that God wouldn't allow the two happy clouds to stay together.

She realized she was biting her fingernails. They were wet and jagged, her fingertips chapped. She had long, lean, beautiful hands, but her fingernails were a total mess. It looked like beavers were trying to use them to make a dam. The nail-biting was a new thing for her. She had just started it within the past two weeks. And she couldn't stop. She didn't even recognize most of the time, when she was doing it. She shoved her hands forcefully down into her coat pockets to keep them away from her teeth.

Then, through a small, crooked window in a tangle of birch branches, she saw his dark blue Mazda make the turn down the lane toward the school. She jumped with joy like a little kid on a trampoline. Her heart raced. Her mind buzzed with all the memories of moments and feelings they had shared together. The feeling of his lips pressed against hers, softly—against her cheek, her neck. The gentle pads of his fingers caressing her skin. Explosions of happiness as she watched his car pull up alongside her. She bent her neck to see his silhouette through the windshield. She rushed at him and pounced as he was still getting out of the car, his knees still bent. She kissed him all over his face, each one like little bursts of fireworks across the sky. And when their lips finally came together like two lost puzzle pieces, it wasn't like fireworks anymore. It was something inside. Something personal, intimate. Something pumping in her blood. Like spirits passing between them and circling around them, and they fell into each other and into a world where they were the last two people on Earth.

Through her coat, Katie felt the gentle press of his hands against her back. Then, his fingers slid up into the tangles of her hair, and then she felt the soft touch of his fingertips against the skin of her neck, and her body fell deeper into him, and there was a quick shiver rushing through her body like a wind shaking the leaves on a tree. One of her hands was on his face.

Two of her fingers straddled his ear. She moved her fingers slowly through his hair and along his neck like she was marking out a route on a roadmap that she had driven many times before.

They kissed for over 11 minutes. I'll spare you the details, but his car was still running and the door open, so there was a bell that kept ringing the whole time. About six minutes into the kiss, Katie became aware of the sound and laughed a little when she thought of the phrase, "your door is ajar." But they never stopped kissing.

Anyway. Eventually, they peeled themselves apart. He tossed all her luggage into the trunk and the backseat and hung garment bags on hooks. Then, he handed her the present he had got for her—Five Guys burgers and fries. They were magically still hot, and she devoured them as he turned the car around and pulled out under the arch.

"Oh my god this is SO good," she shouted with her mouth full of burger. "Thank you, Poopyface."

"You're welcome, Squirrelbutt," he answered.

She wondered at how well he knew her. How on earth did he know exactly what she was craving? It was uncanny. She looked him up and down. He was wearing the light blue sweater with the elbow patches that she had got him for his Birthday and a pair of worn jeans with the hole wearing through at the knee. He looked long and lean stretched out in the driver's seat with one hand casually on the steering wheel. She loved him. She loved his hands. They were elegant—a musician's hands, quick and nimble. His fingers were very long and slender. They moved gracefully like spider legs and tapped out rhythms. At the tips of each finger on his left hand, he had small, hard callouses. Katie could feel them sometimes when he caressed her skin. They felt rough and hard like sandpaper. On his right hand, he kept his fingernails slightly longer for guitar picking. They were thick, tough nails. His hands were strong but gentle. Even just looking at them made her feel loved.

Dave and Katie actually met at church in the nursery playroom when they were both two years old. Neither of them remembers the day they met. Katie's first memory of him, though, is in that nursery. They were making blueberry muffins together in the plastic kitchen set. He kept insisting on adding spaghetti to the strange mix of plastic ingredients Katie was mixing in a bowl. She kept pulling the spaghetti out, and he kept putting it back in. She started to get so mad at him. She was just on the edge of bursting into tears when suddenly she realized how funny it was to put spaghetti in blueberry muffins. And she began to giggle so hard she fell down. "Spaghetti," she gasped out loud between laughs. Dave came over to her and started laughing too, and they rolled on the floor together. When they both finally stopped laughing, they were laying on the gray floor mats together so close their hair was touching. And they both looked up at the same bright white fluorescent lights.

Katie got so caught up in that memory that she forgot about the bit of burger still in her mouth. She had it hid away in her cheek like a squirrel. She swallowed it and took another bite and leaned back in her seat feeling the road pass by underneath them. She closed her eyes and listened to the air rush around the car. The car heater was running too, so the two sounds converged in a surprising, humming harmony. Her heart rate slowed down. They still had a six-hour drive together to get back home. They were scheduled to have dinner with the Ecchols before Dave would drop her off at her parents' house just a few miles away.

It was a little strange that Dave wasn't playing music. He listened to it all the time. They had surprisingly little overlap in their musical tastes. He liked older music from like the 90's and early 2000's—back when he says Christian music was actually good. She liked more contemporary stuff. He liked heavy music with clashing guitars and loud, pounding drums. She preferred gentler instrumentation that spotlighted the vocal melody. But the car was surprisingly quiet. She noticed his fingers drumming on the steering wheel, so he at least had a song going in his head.

Should she tell him now? Should she wait until later in the drive? Her heart was racing again. She had already had the conversation with him like 15 or 20 times in her mind. Sometimes he was very open and understanding, but most of the time he got angry. Even in her fictional account of the conversation.

She swallowed another bite of burger, and a knot of tension rose into her throat. She felt suddenly very hot. She was gonna do it. She could feel the words rising up into her lips. The carefully-curated opening words she had been preparing for months. But they were coming out way too fast. "Do you think it's weird that the church never really recognizes all the work your mom does?" Dave's mom had been the music director at the church for thirty years, since she was seventeen years old. It was a volunteer position.

"What?" Dave legitimately did not understand the words. They all came out wound together like a ball of yarn. And he had been lost in his own thoughts just before she started speaking. But he could tell that she was saying something that was important to her. He could feel the change in the air around them like a proton suddenly shifting its charge out of the blue. Was it a proton? Was that the right word? Why was he even thinking in science metaphors? He hadn't taken a science class of any kind since high school. She started speaking again, much slower this time. Almost too slow.

"Do you think it's weird that the church never really recognizes all the work your mom does," she repeated. As she was speaking, Dave realized that she was saying the words exactly as she had said them the first time. It was an exact replica of her first sentence just slowed down.

"Ummm," he hummed. "I don't know. I mean I don't really think she wants any kind of recognition. She just does it because she believes that God is calling her to do it. She doesn't need anything else."

"I know. But don't you think it's a little disrespectful. Like for example in the church bulletin every week, it lists all of the names of the deacons and the trustees but never your mom's name. And those guys don't even do a fraction of the work your mom does for the church."

He shifted in his seat and it made a kind of farting sound. His face tightened. He didn't really understand what she was getting at. "I guess it would be really nice to put her name in the bulletin, but I don't know if it's disrespectful. I think your dad probably knows that she doesn't really want to be recognized or anything."

Katie's dad was the pastor of the church—Picture Creek Bible Church in Picture Creek, PA. He puts the church bulletin together every Sunday. "It's no coincidence that all the deacons and trustees are men," she continued. "And your mom is a woman. I think there's something disrespectful about it. To all women."

He was shocked. He had no idea she felt this way. Where was it coming from? He shifted his eyes from the road briefly to make eye contact with her. God, she was beautiful. The love of his life. She was his love story—the only love story he would ever know in this life. And he knew that he was her love story too. That was a lot to live up to, but he was ready for the responsibility of it. He knew he could make her happy. It was the thing he cared about most—her happiness.

Her big, round, blue eyes were wide with earnestness. Her big, blonde, curly hair shook in the sunlight that skated over her. He almost couldn't take it he loved her so much. He felt a knot of tension in his chest. He noticed a tension too in the expression on her face—an expectation. She was waiting for him, wanting something from him. There was a still sadness he could see when he looked deep behind her eyes. He wanted to slash it to bits with a sword like a conquering hero. But he could tell she was holding the sadness like a friend. It wasn't her enemy.

"Did you hear what I said," she asked him.

"Yeah." He blinked his eyes back to the road. "Do you think your dad is sexist," he offered.

"No, I don't. Not really. I think it's the church. I think it's a problem with the church."

"Like our church? Or do you mean like all churches?"

"All churches."

"You mean like how women can't be leaders in the church? Like at least in most churches that I know of women can't be pastors or deacons."

"Exactly."

"But they can be missionaries. . ."

"Yeah. In like dangerous parts of the world. But they can't be trusted to be leaders in their own home church. What message does that send to the young women in the church or to the women who are new in their faith . . . that they'll never be good enough. That they're somehow lesser. That's a terrible message. It's not a loving message at all. It doesn't even seem like a Christlike message to me." There was no anger in her voice. Just sadness. And urgency.

"I get it," he said. "I see it too. But there are Biblical precedents and descriptions of who can be leaders in the church."

"It's garbage, though," she responded. "That's like the definition of taking something out of context. All of those precedents come from Paul's letters. And Paul wasn't writing to everyone all across time. He was writing for a specific purpose and a specific audience. He was responding to problems and tensions within the early church. That was his solution to a specific problem in the church. Now, we have different problems. We need different solutions."

He swallowed a hot, dry knot of tensions that kind of sizzled in his gut. She wasn't wrong about that. Slowly, he nodded. "You're right." Last year, he had written a paper for a class on Paul's Letters arguing a very similar point. Katie had read it. He remembered a counterargument that someone in his class posed. It wasn't a great argument at all, but he remembered feeling like it had at least some merit. That when Paul's words to the early Christians being canonized in scripture, they become God's words to all Christians over all time. He thought about that, but he didn't say it. He didn't want to argue with her. He wanted to make her happy.

"Maybe there are some things I can do," he said. "You know, I'll be able to create committees and appoint committee leaders." In just over a month, he would be starting a new job as an Associate Pastor and Worship Leader at a large church in Ohio. They would be moving to a town called Willoughby just a few days after their honeymoon. "And I can recognize the work of the women in the church more openly during services. I can speak encouragingly to the young women in church who want to pursue leadership roles within the church or want to go into the ministry. And maybe someday, we'll get our own church and we can minister differently to the women and have female deacons and trustees. I think those are all good things."

She reached her hand across the console between the two seats and slid her long, thin fingers into his hand, and he wrapped his fingers gently around hers. And they smiled at each other for a moment.

"But I also think," he continued. "That women are doing important things in the church even now, and we shouldn't diminish that. Sunday School teachers, choir directors. Kids' ministry leaders. . ."

She pulled her hand away. Not angrily. Casually. "Of course," she said. "But there also shouldn't be a limit on how a person can minister at a church just because she's a woman."

"I agree," he nodded.

He watched a Dodge Caravan in the other lane slip a little on a patch of ice, so he slowed down, gently. He turned to Katie and noticed that she was staring down at her half-eaten burger.

"Can I have some fries," he asked.

"Sure. Go for it." She sat the paper bag closer to him. He reached in, grabbed a handful, and shoved them all in his mouth. She couldn't help but laugh at his puffed-out cheeks and a stray potato poking out between his lips.

Katie felt beads of sweat starting to bubble on her forehead, and she realized suddenly how hot she felt. She started taking off her coat in the tight space of Dave's Mazda. The seat belt kept locking every time she would turn her shoulders. She had the coat half off and her arms stretched back at strange angles when she stopped struggling and just breathed. She wasn't done with her confession. Not even close. That was just the first phase of her plan, and she knew it was going to be easiest. The hardest part was still to come.

"You ok," he asked her. He reached over and helped her with the coat.

"Yeah. Thanks." Her voice was tired. "Does it ever bother you the way the church treats the LGBTQ community?"

"What do you mean? Our church?"

"I guess I mean the whole church. The church in general. The way that most Christians seem to treat them."

"Cause I was gonna say, there's nobody from that community in our church. Not that I know of."

"And that's part of the problem," she shot back. "They don't feel welcome in churches. In our church. In any church. Because we tell them they're going to hell. We make them feel judged just for being who they are."

Dave was starting to feel like he was being ambushed. "Ok," he started, not knowing what he was going to say next. But the words were coming out anyway. "I agree that anybody who comes into a church should feel loved and welcomed and like they belong. We're all sinners. And we're all God's children. And he loves all of us regardless of what we've done. And the message of Christ is to share that love that God's shares with us onto others. But, I mean, the Bible is clear that homosexuality and sexual perversion and sexual immorality are sinful. And the wages of sin is hell. Everyone should feel loved when they step inside a church, but they should also feel convicted of their sin. Challenged to walk a different path."

"But being gay or transgender or whatever is not a sin."

"How can you say that? I understand the Bible isn't exactly clear on many things, but it's pretty clear on sexual immorality." His voice was rising. He didn't notice, but Katie did.

"Ok," she said. "But it's no worse of a sin than your sin and my sin. And you're an associate pastor at a church. A gay person couldn't be a pastor at your church."

"Well, first of all. It's our church. It's not my church. We both agreed to this job. We prayed over it. We agreed. It's our church. Secondly, a gay person is openly living in sin. Not feeling convicted by the Holy Spirit. Not trying to change. And you can't compare being gay or transgender to being a woman, which is what it seems like you're trying to do. That's not fair to women. There's no sin in being a woman. Women don't choose their gender. It's how they're born." When he finished saying this. He realized that his tone was too harsh. He licked his lips and swallowed dryly. He almost missed the thing that Katie was about to say, because he was busy telling himself to calm down.

"You don't think people are born gay or transgender?"

"No." Calm down, he told himself. "That's not how God made them. Each one of us is fearfully and wonderfully made. We're all image-bearers of God. They, the LGBTQ community, are choosing to pervert that image. Pervert their bodies. And for what? For their own pleasure? For their own sexual gratification? That's the opposite of the teachings of Christ. He taught us to deny ourselves and our sinful nature and to take up our cross. The cross is different for everyone. But to love others. Live a life of service to others. That's where we can gain abundant life. Not from pursuing our own pleasure." He knew she knew this. Of course she knew this. Why was he telling her? Recently, he had taken up an internet hobby late at night on social media and in group chats, trolling on atheists and people who were so-called "deconstructing" their faith. The words that he was saying now were the same words he had been typing to strangers on the internet. But she's not a stranger, he told himself. She's the love of my life.

"So you want them to live alone and miserable? You don't want them to be happy?" Her voice was rising now too.

"Not if happiness means living in sin. If your eye causes you to sin, you should pluck it out." Internally, he was fighting with himself, but these words just kept coming out. He couldn't stop them. He had a sense that some treasure hidden deep inside his heart was being attacked. And it was Katie attacking it. He knew that was what made it all the more scary.

"David. I know all the same Bible verses you know. Don't spout them at me like I don't know them."

"I'm sorry . . . you're right." He nodded. She was right.

"It's ok. But none of that is for us to judge. It's not our place to stand in judgment over them or anyone. Our job is to share Christ's love. To the least of these. Because we all have planks in our own eyes."

He actually laughed a little, breaking the tension. "Now who's spouting verses?"

She didn't laugh but she smiled. "I know. But I think we're both trying to live out our faith and to be true to the Bible. And I think we're just emphasizing different verses and maybe interpreting passages of the same scripture differently."

"I agree," he said. "And that's ok." He took her hand in his and squeezed a little too hard. "It's good. We should challenge each other. We shouldn't agree on absolutely everything. We need to be honest with each other and live life as a team even if we don't always agree. Because we're gonna disagree."

She pushed a spring of hair out of her face and tucked it behind her ear. She took a deep breath out. She wanted so badly to leave the conversation here. It was nice. It was good. They were happy. It was going actually better than she thought it would. But she knew she couldn't stop. He deserved to know the whole truth. They were getting married in exactly one week. He needed to know everything now. She swallowed back her fear. "So then how can we say that the Bible is the inerrant and infallible word of God if it's so unclear that it's gonna cause division within the families, within the church?"

He pulled his hand away and rolled his eyes. "Well, maybe that's all part of God's design. Jesus even warned us that he came to separate sons from fathers and daughters from mothers." It occurred to him suddenly that by taking this tact, he was essentially conceding that the Bible is divisive. And he didn't think he really agreed with that. He stared through the windsheild. Snow was beginning to fall in chubby, wet flakes.

"That sounds like chaos to me. Why would God want that? That's awful. Why would you believe that?"

"I'm not saying there can't be reconciliation. And maybe that's part of the design too. That we find ways to stay together, to live together, to work together as one body even if we can't agree on everything."

"And you think that's the purpose of the Bible?"

"No, I don't."

"The story of Creation for example."

"Ok."

"That can't be literally true, right?"

"I don't know. Why not?"

"Because no one was around to see it. How would anybody possibly know how the universe was made?"

"Well, the words were divinely-inspired. Moses or whoever the writer of Genesis was had some insight or inspiration. A vision like John in the book of Revelation. He was given glimpses of the end times. Why couldn't God have given someone glimpses of the beginning?"

"Do you really think God created the whole universe in six days?"

"The Bible says it. I have no reason not to believe it."

"There are multiple disciplines of science that contradict it, though. Biology, geology, paleontology. They all point to a story that's different from the Genesis account."

"All that stuff is garbage. They find one bone or a tooth or something and they make up an entirely new species. Somehow, they magically know how big the animal was, what it looked like, what it ate, when it lived—all from that one shin bone. It's ridiculous. It's all speculative. It's not science. It's all just theory that can't be tested." He shrugged. "That's not science. Science is about testing your assumptions. How can they test something that happened millions of years ago?"

"So you really think you know better than the smartest, most educated people on the planet who have studied their specific field their whole lives? You're smarter?" She gestured with her hands in large, circular motions. "You know more than all the experts?"

"No! I'm not saying that. But I do think they believe their field and their work is more important than it really is, more authoritative than it really is. That's human nature. You dedicate your life to something, and you build it up so it's flawless. It's all-important. It can do no wrong."

"Don't you think that's true for you too? You see everything through the lens of your faith."

"And you don't?"

"Well. . .I do, but I feel like I'm working on being more open. On being less certain."

"Why? What is that gonna do for you? Why is that better than living by faith?" He didn't know why he was having this conversation with Katie or how the conversation got to this point. He didn't really even mean most of what he was saying. He was just speaking reactively, defensively. From some unthinking part of his brain.

No. Wait. That's exactly what he believes. Every word he said, he believed. It just wasn't coming out right. It didn't sound right. He shook his head.

"I just want to be open and explore," she continued. "I don't want to believe something just because my Dad's a pastor and showed me what to think and how to act. I want to be my own person. And have my own ideas. I wanna figure out who I am without my family."

"Are you deconstructing," he asked tentatively, with a warble in his voice like a pigeon.

"I mean I don't really wanna put a label on it. I think my faith is just changing."

"Gawd dammit, babe," he shrieked. "You are. You're deconstructing." The snow was falling faster, but the road was still mostly clear with just a few windswept patches of snow here and there. "In less than a month, we're gonna be leaders in a church where we've never been to on a Sunday morning. People we don't hardly know are gonna be looking to us for encouragement, guidance, like. . .stability. We gotta be as united as we can be, babe. We'll be in the spotlight." He started shaking his head. His lip doubled over. "I need you." Tears just started gushing. He put his free hand over his face and wiped them away. He collected himself quickly. The tears dried up. "I don't wanna talk about this anymore right now."

"Ok," she said. She was picking at the buttons on her coat. She had slung the coat over her lap after she took it off. She tossed in the back seat. "I'm sorry."

He put his blinker on and took the on-ramp to the highway. Katie knew he preferred driving on the backroads the whole way home. But the highway was faster, of course, so she assumed that he just wanted to get this car ride over as quickly as possible.

Her hands were shaking a little. They felt tingly. She shoved them both under thighs, and they groaned against the leather seat. She felt weak. Tired. She slid down in her seat and took another bite of her burger. It was cold now. Her jaw worked around the burger as she slowly turned her head to look out the window. The snow swirled and circled in the wind. It was lighter now, and the wind was picking it up before it hit the ground. She looked out at the rolling hills of Pennsylvania stretching green and gray all the way to the horizon.

She wondered if she had just ruined her life.

～

Dave pulled his Mazda in under the big maple tree at his parents' house. His dad owned his own engineering firm, so they made a lot of money and owned a big, beautiful home tucked away under a canopy of trees on a 50-acre tract of terraced land with a patchwork of crisscrossing creeks and springs bubbling through it. Dave's dad designed the house himself with four enormous, high-ceilinged rooms in the center of it and a quirky maze of rooms, hallways, and staircases around it. It was truly one of a kind. The light was on over the side deck, and Katie could see all the stunning woodwork even in the dark.

As soon as the engine shut off, Dave lunged out of the car and slammed the door. Katie shivered. The snow was gusting now and falling fast. It was almost 7 o'clock. They had passed the last three hours of the drive in silence. The roads got slicker and more snow-covered the closer they got to home.

Dave walked fast up the front steps to the door. Katie ran to keep up. It was cold. She left her coat in the backseat of the car. She was shivering.

Finally, when they got inside the house, it was warm. The fire was crackling, and the whole house filled with the smell of lasagna. Katie loved Maggie's lasagna, and she realized immediately that her soon-to-be-mother-in-law had made it just for her. She felt like such a fraud. She had so much love in her life, and she felt like she was casting it aside.

She kicked off her shoes and sat alone on the couch over by the fire to warm up. This was her favorite room in the house, with the coziest furniture, the hardwood-paneled walls and ceiling, and the brick chimney. There was a mandolin and fiddle on the mantle and an acoustic guitar on a stand in the corner of the room. This is the room they would all come to after dinner and just jam together. It was magical, really.

But then she remembered how badly she had to pee. She had been holding it for the last three hours of the trip, because she didn't want to ask Dave to pull over. There was a little half-bath in the adjacent room. She went in and locked the door. And she started crying. Out of the blue. Her shoulders were heaving. She spilled out onto the floor, and her face started bubbling with tears and snot.

David could feel the tension in his shoulders and hands and even around his eyes. His teeth were clenching. He was so tired. He wasn't sure if anyone was speaking to him or not. His brothers had come over to see him, because he hadn't been home in months. He was too focused on finishing his thesis. His whole upper body felt heavy. He dropped into a creaky wooden chair at the wood.

He actually appreciated that Katie was thinking and questioning and growing. In some real sense, he was excited for her. He respected Katie completely, and he knew in his heart that her searching was good and holy and all in good faith. But the timing was just so bad. They were getting married in a week. They would be installed as pastors at a strange, new church in just about a month. Now more than ever, they needed to be on the same page. She needed to respect that this was throwing their lives all out of whack and tilting them over and knocking them down. He was afraid.

He heard her gentle footsteps on the staircase coming up from the music room, and a surprising tear suddenly popped over his eyelid and trailed down along his cheek. He couldn't look at her at first. He was too angry. Scared. Confused. Hurt. He flashed away the tear with his finger.

"Katie!" He heard his mother scream. She ran over to Katie and gave her a long, loving hug.

He forced himself to look at Katie, and his heart broke for her. He could see in her face that she had been crying. He didn't want that for her. He wanted for her nothing but joy and love and beauty. Maybe it would be ok. Maybe they could be ok. Make it work. He had to make it work. For her. It had to work. They belonged together. They could make it work.

He felt a lump in his throat. He had no earthly idea if it could work.

They were eating lasagna. His brothers were laughing about some stupid joke that nobody else got. They loved poop jokes. They were both engineers in their dad's firm, and they loved poop jokes more than anything. That explains why they were both still single. In fact, Dave couldn't even remember either of them ever having a girlfriend.

Suddenly, his mom jumped in out of nowhere with, "I'm just so excited for the wedding! It's gonna be so beautiful! I remember when you guys were little, couldn't've been more than four or five. You guys would see each other in church and just start giggling for no real reason. You would just look at each other and laugh. You made each other so happy." Her smile was broad and luminous as she spoke. There were tears of joy charging up behind her eyes. "I'm just so happy!"

His dad laid his hand gently on her back. He wasn't a warm or loving man, but he tried hard. And Dave respected him for it. He was a good father, and Dave expected he was a good husband. He always listened intently. He made you feel loved and cared for even if he never said the words, "I love you" or "I'm proud of you." You always felt it. He was never very good at expressing vulnerability. Even his smiles seemed awkward and forced. There were photos in the hallways with his Dad brandishing strange smiles that made his face look ugly even though he was a very handsome man. Dave always assumed it had something to do with his Dad's childhood. He never met his grandparents, but he had heard stories. They were hard people. Or maybe it was just his dad's way. By nature, he was a cold, hard scientist compelled by logic, reasoning, and mathematics. He came alive when he had a problem to solve. Maybe that was just how he expressed his love for life–through his work, his projects.

Dave stuck his fork in his lasagna but couldn't take another bite.

Katie reached across the table and took Maggie's hand. She was crying again. What a heartwarming story. She wanted so badly to be a good daughter-in-law. She wanted so badly to make everyone happy. Why couldn't she just be the person she was expected to be? What would be so wrong about believing what they all believed?

But then she thought about all the migraine headaches Maggie would get the weeks leading up to holidays and important musical services at the church. She never received any kind of salary for her work at the church, and she had been continually forced into difficult situations by the pastor (Katie's dad) and the elders at the church. They would make demands on her that would go against her philosophy of music ministry and put her directly into confrontational relationships with her singers and musicians—who were also volunteers. She was always fighting to protect all the egos at the church, and she never received any support from the church leaders. She just had to make it work the best she could. Katie had seen too much behind the curtain. She saw the pain it would cause her.

She remembered one Sunday night about six years ago, she witnessed Maggie shaking a handful of Aleve capsules out of a bottle and swallowing them at the water fountain in a dark hallway at the church, and she still forced herself to lead choir practice that night even through the migraine. Katie could see the pain behind her eyes at choir practice. She'll never forget the tension she saw in her eyes and the shakiness in her voice that night. It wasn't right. Something was broken.

"I love you, Maggie," she said across the dinner table. Maggie gripped her hand tighter. They smiled at each other. The light from the chandilier shined in their wet eyes.

"Pffffft," said Luke, Dave's older brother.

"Ew! Who farted," exclaimed his oldest brother, Jonah. The two of them laughed hysterically.

"Shut up," Dave snapped at them, and stared daggers.

~

After dinner, Katie ran back out to Dave's Mazda in the snow. She was shivering. The snow was still falling. The car was covered. Dave turned on the engine and cranked up the heater. He began scraping ice off the windshield.

It was dark. A trail of driveway lights sparkled back to the road like an airport runway. It hurt her eyes to look at them reflected in the rearview mirror. The sound of Dave's scraper against the ice was like fingernails on a chalkboard. Katie felt the sound like a flip and a flop in her chest. The sound of the heater blew in her ears. Those were the only two sounds she could hear. She closed her eyes and swallowed.

"I wanna go home," she whispered. She felt completely alone.

David dropped himself down into the car and tossed the scraper into the backseat. He slammed the door and blew warmth into his freezing hands. He pulled the sleeves of his sweater over his hands and threw the car into reverse. He wanted to say something encouraging to Katie. He could sense that she was hurting, but he had a catch in his throat. He didn't know what it was.

He swung around in his seat to look out the rear window. He backed down the driveway, his Mazda pushing aside the snow. Out on the main road, it seemed impossibly dark. Even the headlights only gave a few feet of visibility. But he knew the roads as well. . .well. . .as well as he knew Katie, which turned out to be not nearly as well as he thought.

He took a turn too fast, and his Mazda fishtailed for a second before finding traction again. He felt Katie tense up in the seat next to him, but she didn't say anything. He slowed down. He heard the engine rev down. He heard the tires crunch in the snow. It was far too quiet, so he turned on some music—Cory Asbury's *Reckless Love*. He didn't really care for the song, but he knew it was one of her favorites. It was a peace offering. They continued in silence.

Eventually, they reached Katie's house. The Mazda slid to a stop in their driveway. Dave jerked on the e-brake to keep it from sliding on the hill. He popped the trunk, and Katie reached for one of her bags.

"I got it," he said. The words came out of his mouth more violently than he had intended. She pulled her hand back quick and slipped in the ice but righted herself with a hand on the bumper. He grabbed her backpack and slung it over his shoulders and then weighed himself down with all of her luggage, one bag at a time, until he looked like a refugee waiting to steal away in the night. The weight of all her bags made him feel sad. For a moment, he couldn't catch his breath from the sadness.

But he managed to trudge through the snow up the hill to the back porch. He struggled up the back steps, but he didn't want her to see him struggling. He was aware of the feeling—the feeling that he didn't want to be struggling. The feeling that he hated for her to see the struggle. He slipped in the ice on the second step and nearly fell. Her largest spinner bag propped him up.

Katie said nothing. She lept up the stairs ahead of him and opened the door. He looked up at her. He watched the porch light twist and play through her curly, blonde hair like a creek bubbling through a cascade of stones. Her face looked hard striped in shadow. He breathed out slow then proceeded to scoot passed her and squeeze in through the doorway. "Thank you," he murmured.

Once inside, he dropped her bags to the floor. They skidded over the linoleum. He wiped his snow-crusted shoes on the braided jute rug. The kitchen was small and minty green with a brand-new refrigerator about three sizes too big for the room. It smelled like lavender. Katie's mom was really into essential oils. In the dim light, he could see the curve of the mist rising from the diffuser by the sink.

"I'm sorry I dropped your bags," he said to Katie, turning slightly.

"It's ok. Thanks for schlepping it through the snow." She took his coat and hung it up on the coatrack in the

adjoining dining room.

"There they are!" It was Katie's dad coming up the stairs from the basement. They had a half-finished basement, with a study and a small, dank, Pittsburgh bathroom. "How was the trip?"

"Hey, Dad," Katie said. "It was fine."

"Hi Pastor Vreeland. How are you?"

"Oh. Blessed and highly favored. Leave the bags," Pastor Vreeland said quickly, adjusting his glasses. "We'll get 'em later. Come on in the living room."

The three of them walked through the kitchen together and out into the living room. The living room was small, but it looked even smaller with all the bookshelves along the walls, framing in the windows. Dave heard the rocking chair creak over the wood floor before he saw Katie's mom. There she was in her antique rocking chair, which supposedly her grandfather built for her grandma way back in the day, rocking in her usual spot over by the radiator. She was knitting.

"Hi, Mrs. Vreeland," David said quietly.

"Hey, Mom."

"Hello there," Mrs. Vreeland smiled. "Please have a seat." The rocking chair never stopped creaking. The tv was on, but the volume was turned nearly all the way down. It was mostly just a glow in the corner of the room.

David also took notice of Pastor Vreeland's train set, which he sets up for Christmas the day after Thanksgiving every year. It takes up over half the living room. He sets up six or eight folding tables and covers them with some kind of white cottony fabric that looks like snow. Then, he creates this whole pre-WWII, midwestern town with beautiful porcelain houses, churches, banks, bakeries, barns, etc. He's got little figurines of children skating on a pond and moms and dads going to work or getting groceries. And then the locomotive chugs along around and around, over bridges, and around the tree farm. It's a spectacular set up.

"Your train set looks awesome this year," he told his soon to be father-in-law.

"Thanks."

David had even forgotten that it was mid-December. His family doesn't ever decorate or even talk about Christmas until the last minute, and then they leave up the decorations through the end of January.

He moves some magazines off the couch and places them on the floor so he can sit down. The couch creaks when he sits down. The upholstery is all chewed up. They have a cat named Max who likes to chew and claw at all their furniture. Everything in the house looks old and out of date.

Katie sits down next to him on the couch, but she leaves some room between them. A static charge passes between them when she seats down, but they don't really notice it.

"It's so good to have you both home." Pastor Vreeland sat in his burnt orange recliner. He was still holding a paperback book with his finger shoved inside to mark the page. "How did everything finish up for you at school?"

David cleared his throat. "Good. I successfully defended my thesis. There was this big conference room in the library. One whole wall was all windows, and I kept looking out at the snow in the trees and thinking, I can't wait for this all to be over so I can come home and get married and we can start our lives together."

"Praise God. Praise God," sat Pastor Vreeland. "What was your thesis about?"

"Uh. It was about how the early Christians established the New Testament canon, and. . ."

Katie unplugged from the conversation. She had heard him talk about his thesis so many times, she knew exactly what he was going to say, probably word for word. She caught herself biting her lip and made herself stop. Oh, that stupid rocking chair. It's so loud on the hardwood floor, and it's wearing on the floor. Why won't she just put a rug under it or something?

She knew her mom was in pain all the time. And the rocking chair helped her somehow and the heat from the radiator. Even the knitting helped keep her fingers from tightening up. She knew all that and respected it, but it still annoyed the crap out of her.

She had a flash of a thought that the reason it annoyed her so much is because it's a picture of her future, 25-ish years from now. Why wouldn't she inherit her mother's arthitic bones? She knew she was doomed to be just like her mother. And she loved her mother. It wasn't a bad thing, exactly. But then again, her blonde hair came from nowhwere. Her parents both have straight, brown hair. The mystery of blonde curls defies all science. So maybe she's some kind of an outlier, and she'll never develop arthritis. She would pray for that.

Where's Max? She looked around but didn't see him. He was getting older, and he liked to be by himself more and more in his old age. Katie could respect that. She just wanted to curl up in bed under her favorite blanket with some hot chocolate and read a book.

Finally, the conversation ended, and Dave helped her carry her bags up to her room. Her room was up in the half-finished attic. There was a surprise staircase sort of cut out of the hallway that leads up to her room. Even though her room is very spread out, it feels very small. Katie thought it was cozy. It had sloped ceilings, and it was sectioned off into two parts as it sort of wrapped around the stairwell.

Dave placed the last piece of luggage beside her bed.

"Thank you," she told him.

"No problem." He cracked his knuckles. "How's your mom. She looked tired."

"She's in pain all the time. It wears her out. The arthritis is advancing, and her medication isn't working as well as it was. She's going to see the doctor after the Holidays, and he's gonna try a new medicine."

He nodded. "Good. Good. I hope this one works."

"Me too."

He nodded again or maybe he was still nodding from the first time. "Well. . .I better go before the roads get any worse. But I'll see ya tomorrow at church?"

"Yeah."

He kind of pointed at her and made little shooting motions with his hands. Why would anyone do that?

19

"Bye," he waved. And he started walking down the steps. She could hear his feet touch each step, and she felt the distance growing between them.

～

It was late. Katie was curled up in her bed under her favorite blanket. Her Mom knitted it for her. She sipped her hot cocoa and settled into her pillow. She was reading *The Universal Christ* by Richard Rohr on her cell phone. She flicked her finger to turn the page. The glow from her phone lit up her face in the dark and dazzled in her eyes. The book was mind-blowing, revolutionary for her. But she knew that Dave probably wouldn't like it. And that made her kind of sad.

Suddenly, her phone buzzed. He was calling. She leaned up on her elbow and swallowed. She flicked her finger to answer. "Hello," she said and immediately wished she could take it back and start her greeting over again. She would say it happier, warmer. The way she said it sounded like it would have if she was getting a call from an insurance company or something. She cleared her throat.

"Hey."

He sounded tired. He breathed out heavy and the rush of the sound hit her ear. She wanted to hug him. She felt tears started to crystallize behind her eyes. "Hey," she said back, softer, lighter—like a wisp of breath on a cold day that unravels in the air and disappears.

"I'm really sorry, baby," he said. "I didn't respond well today at all. I feel bad, because I know it was hard for you to tell me those things. And I should've been more supportive. The stuff I was saying earlier today wasn't really what I wanted to say. I'm not sure how it happened, but the conversation got away from me. I guess I was kind of confused and maybe a little hurt, and I just started spouting of stupid stuff that I didn't even really mean."

"No. It's ok." She stood up and began pacing around the room. "It's hard. This is hard. And I should've talked to you about this a long time ago."

"Why didn't you? I mean, I think that's the hardest thing is I think this must've been going on for like a long time with you. And it's like it was some big secret or something. I just wish we would've been talking about this all along, you know."

"I know," she said. A tear slipped down her cheek. "I'm sorry. I should've. You're right. I should've told you about it a long time ago. We could've talked about it."

"It's ok."

"I just. I guess I was just afraid. I didn't know how you were gonna take it. I thought you'd be mad at me."

"No. I'm not mad. Of course I'm not mad. But I didn't take it very well. I'm mad at myself, really. Not mad at you." After a short pause, he added, "But we're in this together, you know. We have to share big things with each other. No matter what. Ok? And I can't shut down like I did today. That's not helpful. We gotta stay open with each other. We gotta talk it out."

"Yeah," she said through tears. "Ok." She wiped her face with her sleeve.

"Hey," he started.

"Yeah?"

"I know it may seem like I'm fighting with you. But I don't think that's what I'm actually, like, trying to do. I think maybe I'm trying to fight *for* us. You know. I don't really know how to explain it."

"I think it get it," she said. "And I think that's exactly what I'm trying to do too."

"And," he added, sharply. "I think you have more to say. Am I right about that?"

"Yes."

"Then let's talk it out. . ."

"Right now?"

"It doesn't have to be now."

"Not now. Tomorrow."

"Ok. I promise I'll listen. And I'll try to stay open to whatever journey you're on."

"Thank you."

"I love you, Squirrelbutt!"

"Love you too, Poopyface."

"Bye."

"Oh. Hey. Do you wanna go for a run tomorrow morning," she asked.

"It's like 24 degrees outside."

"So? You a wussy?" She laughed and sniffled, still crying a little.

"Oh, I'm no wussy. I'll see you tomorrow morning. Love you, baby. Bye Bye Have a good night." There was no need for him to ask what time or where are we gonna run or where do you wanna meet. Dave and Katie had known each other their whole lives, and they had developed a bit of telepathy when it came to certain things. Over the past summer, they actually ran a marathon together in Pittsburgh, and they had negotiated a workout routine that they both approved of. Katie still didn't have her own car, so Dave would come to her house. She also lived on a better road for running. There was light traffic, beautiful countryside to look at, and challenging hills to navigate. And always at 7:05 am.

"Ok. Bye." She hung up the phone. She wiped her face again with her sleeve. She couldn't remember how many times she cried today. She was an adult woman now. This amount of tears was unacceptable. She crawled in under her blanket on the bed, wiped her face one more time, and fell fast asleep.

Chapter 2

Sunday

DAVE PULLED INTO KATIE's driveway at exactly 7:04am the next morning. She was already stretching out in the yard, and she looked both cute and sexy in her tights, oversized hoodie, red wool scarf, and her thick headband that covered her ears. Her hair was pulled back into a big, puffy ponytail.

"It's so cold," he told her as he stepped out of the car and pulled his knit cap down over his ears. It was a Steelers cap with a big, puffy ball on top to kind of match her ponytail.

They stretched together for a few minutes and then took off down the road. They turned left, which led through windy roads, steep hills, and beautiful farm country. Dave wished they were going right, which was a much easier route, but Katie was leading the way, so he just went along for the ride. He could see the mist of her breath in the cold tangle with his for a moment and then vanish into the sky. And he thought of Ecclesiastes. "Hevel. Hevel. Everything is Hevel." Hevel is a Hebrew word. Most translations interpret the word as "Meaningless." But hevel actually means mist or vapor—a temporary, fleeting vapor like breath that you expend. In a moment, it's gone. That's life, at least according to the Teacher.

Anyway, the sky was a deep blue, and there was no wind. It was a peaceful morning. He watched a single deer on the horizon, bending to nibble at some grass. You have to breathe life in as deeply as you can, because each moment tumbles into the next and before you know it, it's gone.

He sped up a bit to catch Katie and run alongside her. She had a long, easy stride and always made running seem effortless. She had been a four-year Cross-Country runner at Messiah College and had placed runner-up at the Conference Championships her senior year. Dave was no slouch either. He had been a state-qualifier in high school in the two-mile. But he still knew that Katie was the better runner, and he had to push to keep up with her.

For a while, they ran in silence and just took in the view and felt their bodies working together in rhythm. After a long time, he knew he had to risk a conversation about her changing faith. It was the only way this was going to work. And probably the only way that lifelong relationships work, especially between men and women. That's what he had read at least in blog posts last night that open communication is always the right course of action in a marriage. After long moment, he finally said, "I wanna clarify something I said yesterday. I want the LGBT community to be happy. Of course I do, but more than that I want them to have joy. And joy comes not by pursuing your own passions and desires. Because those are fleeting. Like a vapor. Like a breath. Joy comes from living a life of service to the people around you. A Christlike love for other people. That's what brings joy."

"I know," she said, turning her face at him to meet his eyes. "David, you're a kind soul. You're a good person. But look at the church. Look at how the church treats the gay community. Why would a gay person or a transgender person ever want to step foot in a church that makes them feel so judged?"

"But what church are talking about? Are you talking about our church?"

"I'm talking about THE Church. The Evangelical churches of America."

"I just don't understand what that means."

"Well, ok. Let's look at our church. You remember Samantha Woods? She was in our Sunday School class when we were in middle school. She started out in youth group with us?"

"Yeah. Sammi."

"Yeah. She's gay. And when her parents found out, they refused to let her come to church anymore. Because she started dressing differently, and she refused to wear the clothes that they thought were appropriate for church. For months, my dad went over to their house several times a week. I don't have any idea what he said to them, but he came back all mopey and salty. And he didn't want me to talk to Sammi anymore. That was his solution. We're not talking to her anymore. When that's the opposite of what she needed. She needed to feel loved. Not judged. Why couldn't he have just said to the congregation. Sammi is our sister in Christ. I mean, she was baptized just like I was. She walked up to the altar and gave her life to Christ just like I did. Why couldn't he just say this is our sister in Christ, and we will love her?"

He blinked at her. "Well, I didn't know any of that. I thought. . ." He shrugged. "I thought she just stopped coming." He shook his head. "But all we can do is love them. We can't care about what the church (air quotes) does or what the people in a church do. We can only control how we treat people."

"But David. Our new church, New Hope Church, I've seen their website. They have a loud stance on homosexuality and transgenderism. You're gonna be leading their youth worship team, and I'm gonna be singing in it. And there are gonna be kids coming up to us and asking us for help. In a very vulnerable time in their lives. And they're gonna think that we have, like, spiritual insight or whatever. And we're gonna have to tell them what the church believes, because we represent the church."

He shook his head and breathed out a puff of air. "Yeah. You're right that we have to let them know what the church believes, but that doesn't mean that we can't love on them and make them feel welcome. You and I, we're not puppets of the church. We're our own people. We can treat everyone with love. That's what Christ would do."

"But then what if we're doing exactly that, and your lead pastor comes to us privately and tells us that we have to handle the situation differently? Less lovingly."

"We can't know that's going to happen. We have to live in faith that things are going to work out for good for those who love God and are called according to His purpose."

"But what if it does happen? Are we gonna quit the church? And then what? Where are we gonna go?"

"But why are you so focused on the negative? Think about all the good that we'll be able to do. All the people we can share the love of Christ with. Fill up their love tank."

"I just think it's naïve to believe that we're not going to run into conflict with church leadership over this issue."

"I don't think that. There's gonna be conflict. That's unavoidable. Why didn't you bring any of this up before? Our interview process was like two months long. You were there with me in the two zoom interviews. You never asked any questions. Never talked to me about it. We've made the decision now. You know, the decision's done. I just feel like we should've talked about this months ago."

She looked away, and he took the time to look down at his shoes gliding over the pavement.

"You're absolutely right," she said finally. "I'm sorry I didn't talk to you about it before. I guess. . .I was just scared, you know. Confused. And too. . .it was a great opportunity for you. I didn't want to ruin it for you or discourage you from taking the job. It's a great opportunity."

"It is. It's a great opportunity. An opportunity for us. They hired both of us. You and me. You had every right to voice your opinion and ask questions. . ."

"David, they asked me three questions the whole time. And one was about having a baby. . ."

"I thought that was a sweet question, actually."

"It was kind of sweet. But my point is that they didn't care what I had to say. They didn't even invite me to the in-person interview."

"You were invited. You just had to work that day."

"I didn't feel invited. They didn't care what I had to say."

"Well, baby, I care what you have to say."

"I know you do," she smiled at him, tiredly. "I appreciate you for that. And I definitely should have talked to you about this earlier. You're right about that, absolutely. I guess I'm just trying to explain why I didn't."

"I know, and I respect it. But I just think . . . moving forward . . . we both need to be more open and honest with each other. Even if it's hard. I trust that we can both find ways to talk to each other even about things that might be a little sensitive."

They turned around at the main road, and started back up the hill. They ran in silence for a long time. Their breaths got shorter and heavier. Louder. And filled the space around them with sound as they worked their way up the long, steep hill.

Finally, the road leveled out for the long, straight stretch back to Katie's house. But they were both still breathing too heavy for conversation. So they finished the run lost in their own thoughts. When they got back to Katie's house, they stretched together against the big oak tree in the yard for a few minutes to cool down.

"Will you pick me up for church later," she asked. "I'd rather ride with you than my parents. You know my Dad likes to get there like three hours early."

"Sure. Pick you up at 10:30?" He could tell she had a lot on her mind. He could read it in her face. He knew she had more she wanted to tell him. And he knew she would tell him eventually. He trusted that she would. He just had to be patient. This is was her story to tell, and he needed to let her do it her way. He never thought he could ever be afraid of her, but he was. In this moment, he was afraid of what the rest of her story might be. And he wanted to know all of it right now. But part of him didn't want to know it at all.

"Ok." She turned her back and started walking up to the house. He watched her ponytail bounce with each long stride up the hill. Then, she turned back to him. "I love you," she told him.

"Love you too."

~

Katie was still getting ready for church when she heard the knock at the back door. She was sitting at her desk in her room, looking in the mirror. Then, she turned and looked around the room. It had been such a sweet and cozy and special spot for her when she was a teenager. But now, it just seemed impractical for a grown woman. She had outgrown the space somehow. It was in some ways a large space. It was spread out. There was quite a bit of floor space all the way around. But in some ways, it was a doll house. The sloped ceilings made it seem small. And the stairwell cut out so much of the floor space. It was awkward. Still a special spot but also kind of annoying.

Suddenly, she jumped up, bounded down the stairs, and ran for the back door. She threw open the door, flung her arms around Dave's neck, and kissed him. It was a deep, loving kiss. A reckless kiss. That they both fell into deeply. The windchimes on the porch rang out a simple melody for them. And they kissed for several minutes.

Finally, their lips slipped apart, and they looked at each other through dazzling eyes.

"Hi," he said.

"Hi." She smiled. "I gotta get my shoes. Hold on."

She ran out of the room and up her staircase. She grabbed a pair of light, blue flats and slid them on. Then, she leapt down the steps, her hair bouncing. Dave was wearing a shirt and tie like he always does to church. She didn't really like the tie. She couldn't figure out exactly why. She locked the back door, and they creaked down the old porch steps together.

He held the car door open for her. She laughed at him. And they went off down the road.

"What do you think about all the violence in the Old Testament and all the passages where God commands the Israelites to murder all the men, women, and children and wipe out entire people groups?"

"Well, good morning to you, too," he laughed.

She didn't laugh. She just smiled at him expectantly.

"Well," he began. He shrugged his shoulders. "It was a violent time. The Bible was written thousands of years ago. Humans were different back then. We can't judge them using our, like, present-day version of morality."

"No," she said quickly. "I'm saying if we believe the Bible is the true and infallible word of God, then I don't know how we can avoid believing that God literally and directly killed 99% of the human population in the flood. Men, women, and children. He killed the entire Egyptian army in the Red Sea after the Israelites crossed through. God Himself murdered people in the Old Testament and ordered the Israelites to murder entire people-groups."

"I don't understand it, babe," he said quietly. "But if you look at the New Testament, it's all about love. Jesus was about loving your neighbor and your enemy. That's the new covenant. We're not under the old covenant anymore. Maybe the old covenant was bloody and violent. But the new covenant is beautiful, loving."

"But it's the same God. If God is unchanging, then how can you explain it?"

"Well, I don't have all the answers, but one thing I do know. I heard on a podcast recently. You know, all the cultures of the ancient world had a flood story. And you know, it was a primitive time. And most of the stories are all mostly about the gods just sort of smiting all the humans, you know? Just mowing 'em all down. Playing with them like a bunch of kids with, like, GI Joes or something in a sandbox. No love. No grace. No forgiveness. Just power. But the Noah story ends with redemption for humanity and a promise from God to never destroy the earth like that ever again." He stopped and licked his lips. "So I guess what I'm saying is that maybe God didn't change. People changed. And it just, like, took humans all that time to be ready for the true story, the true unveiling of a loving God. God had to invest in the Israelites for thousands of years to make humanity ready."

He turned into the church parking lot, which was covered with snow. The snow crunched and moaned under their tires.

Ben Kipling is a local farmer who attends the church occasionally. Every Sunday in the winter, he trams his Kubota down the road, shovels out the church parking lot, and throws down some salt. And he does it for free, which is amazing. The problem is that the church parking lot is all gravel, so he has to leave a thin layer of snow otherwise he would be kicking up all the gravel and spreading it all around.

Before the church built a large addition to their building a few years ago, including classroom space, a youth center, and a children's play area, they launched a fundraising campaign that lasted for three years. After they had raised all the money, they discovered that the cost of building materials had nearly doubled since the time of the original estimate. They had just celebrated the successful completion of their fundraising project with a big party at the church, so instead of waiting to build and continuing to raise funds, the Deacons of the church decided to go ahead and build anyway but cut costs wherever they could. A gravel lot saved them thousands of dollars over a concrete one. Choosing the gravel lot enabled them to move ahead with plans for a big, beautiful back deck that overlooks Picture Creek. Everybody loves the deck, but it never stops them from complaining every Sunday about the gravel lot.

Dave parked the Mazda way in the back of the lot under a pine tree. When he put the car in park, Katie placed her hand over his. She looked him dead in the eyes.

"Do you really believe that people are that evil," she asked. "That we are that evil?"

He shrugged.

"Do you really wanna devote your life to a belief like that?"

"Yes." He snatched his hand away and lunged out of the car.

She ran to catch up to him in the parking lot. She reached for his hand, and he took it, gently. "I believe in us," she told him quietly in his ear as if the wind would blow the words away.

He turned to her, and their noses almost touched. He smiled. "Me too." They walked into the church hand in hand.

The heavy, wooden doors of the Picture Creek Evangelical Church pushed open, and the entrance way buzzed with Sunday morning anticipation. They both shook off the cold. The warmth of the church blushed their faces a gentle red. Their eyes floated up and up and up into the high, vaulted cathedral ceilings. The deep, bellowing sound of the pipe organ churned out a song that neither of them recognized. Picture Creek Evangelical was the largest church in the whole county, and even while all the other churches around were dying off and closing their doors or just barely hanging on, Picture Creek was thriving.

Dave wiped his boots on the woven rug in the entrance way, and salt pellets scattered over the rug and onto the hard wood floors. There were wet footprints tracking everywhere in all directions. Many were clear and wet and well-defined like fresh stamps—a wet, slippery maze of them crossing and twisting. Dave picked up his foot slowly, and flakes of snow shook loose and melted. He watched as his shoeprint slowly dissolved away into the others. He looked down perplexed with one foot raised slightly off the floor.

Katie unwound the scarf her mother had knitted for her and crammed it into her coat pocket, but the red edges of it still popped out and dangled from her black coat like the carcass of a dead puppet. She pulled off her gloves and she could smell the leather. She stamped her feet on the rug.

Neither of them had set foot in the sanctuary for almost a year, but everything about the place was immediately familiar—the smell of the old wood pews mixed with the coffee brewing in the side hall, the way the voices echoed from the stone walls, the way the sunlight slanted through the stained-glass windows.

They moved without thinking, still hand in hand, through a crowd of people. David grabbed two bulletins from a lectern and handed one to Katie. Mrs. Rosemoor noticed them and unfolded a blistering smile. She pounced on them with an awkward hug.

"Ooooooh," she shrieked. "I'm so happy for you two! I can't wait for Saturday!" Her crispy hair slid against their faces, and she smelled strongly of lavender. "I told Abner, I'm just so excited about the two of you getting married. I just never met a couple that's more in love than the two of you!"

Soon, they were surrounded by a throng of old friends and acquaintances, and they were buried in shovelfuls of well wishes and happy, empty phrases and hugs and handshakes.

Eventually, they managed to untangle from the group, and they moved through the pews as one person. The pipe organ had stopped, and everyone was taking their seats. Dave and Katie slid into an empty pew and sat down near the back of the church.

"Hey!"

They both looked up, a bit startled. Dave's mom was suddenly standing beside them. When she leaned toward them, her face was inches from their Katie's face. Katie jumped.

"Ooooh. I'm sorry," Dave's mom said. "I didn't mean to startle you." She laughed awkwardly, then continued. "We don't have any special music scheduled for this morning. Would you two like to sing something for us? I know I'm putting you on the spot, but I'm sure you have a song you could bust out and sing just perfectly."

"Uh. . ." Katie did not want to do it. She and Dave hadn't sung together in months.

"Sure. We'll do it," Dave smiled. Katie turned at him quick with wide, questioning eyes.

"Great," said Dave's mom. "I'll let your dad know," she said to Katie. "David, your old guitar is still in the back room if you want it. But feel free just to use Justin's if you like. He leaves up on stage." And then she walked down the aisle to lead the worship team.

Katie turned to Dave. "I don't wanna do it. Why did you say yes?"

He shrugged. "It'll be fun!" He revealed a disarming smile. "It'll be a hoot," he added, laughing at his word choice. "And there are like a hundred songs we could do by heart."

She turned away and started clicking her fingernails together, a nervous habit she picked up when she was a teenager. But she said nothing.

"Hey, bruh," came a loud splat of a voice from behind them.

Dave spun around in the pew and hopped to his feet. "Giddy! Man! Hey, brother!"

The two old friends clasped hands and then crashed together in a bear hug. The fabric of their coats slid against each other with a gross kind of raspy sound like a stack of stink bugs that spilled over, clattering and scratching over linoleum flooring. And they both started laughing for no apparent reason.

Gideon was a self-proclaimed theobro, with, he claims, a touch of CTE from his football days, which he believed excused him to make weird and inappropriate comments. He had a degree in Theology and owned his own Tree/snow plowing Business. He and Dave grew up together in the church, and they went to the same school. They even played football together in Junior High. Dave, who graduated at just 145 pounds, had been too small to play in high school, but Gideon went on to be an All-Conference linebacker. He even played D-III college ball at Grove City College and was a four-year starter. He and Dave see each other only twice a year. They never call, rarely text, but when they finally come together in the same room, it's like not a single day has passed.

Gideon pushed away out of the hug and nearly knocked Dave over.

"Dude," he shouted, and gave his friend the finger guns. "I am hyped (he sort of howled the word "hyped") for your wedding, man! It's gonna be epic! And the batch party's gonna be so dope. You're gonna love it, dude! I'm serious. Katie. . .!" His voice went up at the end there like a fire alarm. He pivoted his eyes at her. "What's up, dude," he told her. He reached out his arms for a hug.

After a slight pause, she slowly stood up and gave in. His hug was just a little too tight for her comfort. "Hey, Giddy," she said. "How's it going?"

He pushed out of the hug. His eyes snarled at Katie and then at Dave. "You two are gonna bang," he said. "Like. . .soon. You're gonna make sweet, sweet love." He paused a moment to hump the wooden pew. "And have so many babies," he added. "So many beautiful, shy little cherubs toddlerin' around. I can't wait! So excited for you guys! Seriously." Then, he placed his palms together as if in prayer and bowed slightly to them. He pivoted his gaze at Dave. "Wanna hang later? Text me."

Dave nodded, though he was suddenly weirded out by how similar the words "hang" and "bang" sound. Gideon disappeared to the far side of the sanctuary to sit with his parents and his sister.

"I can't believe you're still friends with that guy," Katie said, but she had a big smile on her face. Gideon was hard to like. But he was also hard not to like. But. . .if you really searched your soul, deep down, you have to like Gideon. No matter how much he annoys you or makes you feel uncomfortable, you still want to be around him.

Dave shrugged. He took his coat off and set it on the pew. Katie handed him her coat, and he set it on top of his. Her scarf slipped out of the pocket and dropped to the floor. He bent down to pick it up, and when he came back up, the worship music had started.

Dave's mom kicked off the music with a ripping melody on the mandolin. Soon, the rest of the band joined in, and everyone in the congregation rose to their feet, clapping. The lyrics were projected up on two large screens at the front of the sanctuary. When Dave's mom starting singing, her clear, pristine voice soared over the sound of everything else.

Dave noticed that the worship band had gotten tighter over the past few years. They added a drummer, which probably helped to keep everyone together. But it was a strange choice, because the worship was very bluegrass-y. There was a mandolin, fiddle, guitar, banjo, and bass, and even though the drums didn't quite match the twang of the other instruments, it somehow worked. And there's no doubt that the worship band was a big reason that the whole church was thriving while all the other churches in the community were dying. The music was fun and free and inspiring. It could be sad too, but always with a few rays of sunshine. And the harmony vocals were as beautiful and compelling as ever. Dave's Mom had a way with harmonies, especially vocal harmonies. She arranged all of the music for the worship herself and taught every musician their parts. It was relentless and demanding work, but a work of pure love for her. She never complained about waking up at 4am to work out arrangements in the quiet of her music room. She never complained about taking time off of work to meet a musician at the church for additional practice time. She never complained when a musician made the same mistakes over and over or failed to grasp the subtle dynamics or transitions of her arrangements. She demanded perfection from herself but gave infinite grace to those who worked with her.

The song drifted into the bridge, and it sounded almost jazzy with big, strange chords and crooked time signature shifts. And then the song just melted easily back into the chorus. Dave so missed playing with his mom's worship band. And it made him incredibly excited by the opportunity to start his own worship band as the Worship Pastor at his new church. What an honor it would be to carry on his Mom's legacy. A single tear popped on his eyelash and slid down along his cheek. He wiped it quickly away. He reached for Katie's hand, and she took it, gently. Her hand was warm and tender. It felt like home somehow, and he felt the stresses of life dissolve from his shoulders like a great burden being lifted. He closed his eyes and breathed. He felt his heartbeat in his fingers. He felt each breath fill his lungs. His chest expanded and contracted, and he became intensely aware of the unconscious rhythms of his own body. And then he felt Katie's heartbeat through her fingertips. And the cadence of their heartbeats became as one. And even with his eyes closed, he saw all of the beautiful stained-glass windows—the scene of Jesus as the good shepherd with the lambs running beside him and his gentle hand guiding them. His gentle voice reminding them each of his great love.

"The hungry sheep look, and are not fed." He heard the gentle voice say to him. He remembered the line from a book he had read many times. A.W. Tozer's *The Pursuit of God*. He read that book at least once a year. The next line in the book he remembered was something like, "It is a solemn thing, and no small scandal in the Kingdom, to see God's children starving while actually seated at the Father's table." Tozer was talking about the lack of true worship in churches today. He lamented that churches had shifted their focus so drastically toward correct doctrine and had moved away from a kind of true, reverent worship where you can know God truly and deeply from the very center and core of your being, where your own heart and God's will align like stars.

"The Bible is not an end in itself," he recalled another line from the book, "but a means to bring men to an intimate and satisfying knowledge, that they may enter into Him, that they may delight in His presence, may taste and know the very God Himself in the core and center of their hearts." That was true worship. That was what Dave was experiencing right now. That was his calling to carry out in his new role as Worship Pastor in his new church. And he felt the weight of the responsibility of that, but at the same time, he didn't actually feel it at all. "My yoke is easy. My burden is light." He could trust in God to take care of it. He only had to give it to God.

And he would do it all with Katie by his side . . .

When he opened his eyes, the music was over. Katie's dad was up front, giving the announcements. Then, he told one of his trademark stories, which he probably read in a book somewhere or saw on the internet. After that, he bowed his head and stretched out his hand to pray.

When Katie's dad began to pray and everyone in congregation had bowed their heads and closed their eyes, Katie and Dave snuck out of their pews and headed up toward the stage. It felt strange and powerful to be up and walking around while everyone else in the building was sitting still.

Dave ducked into the side room to grab his acoustic guitar. Through the closed door, Katie heard him quickly tuning his instrument. Then, just as the prayer was wrapping up, he emerged from the room. She swallowed dryly and licked her lips and clicked her fingernails together. She still had no idea what song they were about to sing. She worried if maybe Dave didn't either. She worried they would mess up in front of everybody. She didn't want to disappoint her dad. She felt a bead of sweat slashing down along her cheek.

She grabbed the microphone from the mic stand and clutched it near her breast with both hands. She ventured a glance over at Dave, and he was actually smiling. She was scared to death. He was cool as ice.

Suddenly, he began fingerpicking his guitar. By just the second note, Katie knew exactly what song he was playing. And she knew exactly when she would need to come in. She could even feel the first note already singing somewhere in the back of her mind. It all just felt right and safe. When she starting to sing, the notes and words slipped easily from his lips. It was all smooth and easy like a sailboat skipping over the water.

When Dave came in with his vocal harmony, she felt supported. It made her braver, bolder. She sang with even more power in her voice. He was uplifting her somehow. She felt free. She looked down over the faces of the congregation. Most of the faces, she recognized. She knew them very well. She had looked at their faces many times, had heard them laugh and cry and tell stories, had been over to their houses for meals and parties. She felt connected. She felt cared about. She felt loved.

She looked up into the rafters of the sanctuary. She felt there was a presence, a spirit up in the rafters. She couldn't see it. She could feel it. But it was like seeing. She held out the final note of the song, and she could feel Dave's harmony note blend with her melody. She felt it more than she heard, though she could hear it too, but it was feeling of his note, his voice being inside of her chest and sliding up into her throat and out through her lips. It was a powerful feeling.

When the song was over, she moved over to him and gave him a big hug, melting into him. His strong arm draped around her shoulder and drew her in. And she felt loved. He was right. About the song. She didn't want to do it. But he was absolutely right. She felt that she could trust him. In the hard times. She could count on him. He would lead her in the right direction. She felt connected to him. She loved him.

After the song was over, Dave felt weird. He felt a little queasy, actually. Did she believe what she was singing about, he wondered. Did they believe the same things about the meaning of the song? Would they agree on anything moving forward? How could work together as a couple if they couldn't agree on anything. He tried to push away the thoughts.

He felt her hair brush against his cheek. He felt her shoulder bones under his fingers. He felt her leaning into him in a kind of reckless way, in a completely trusting way. And he heard the congregation clapping for them. The song had gone really well. It was even better than he had anticipated. Maybe this could work, somehow, against all reason. Against all hope. Maybe they were just meant to be together. Like the branches of a tree growing in opposite directions.

～

After the church service, Dave and Katie went out to lunch with their families at Chatterly's. Chatterly's was just outside of Picture Creek about three miles passed the bridge on Bear Hollow Road. It was in the middle of nowhere in a big, old Victorian house set back in behind the pines. There was a pond out back and a greenhouse where many of the vegetables for the restaurant were grown.

Nothing very memorable really happened at that lunch for Dave and Katie, except for one moment that Dave will never forget. After ordering, he had gone off to the bathroom to wash his hands. When he came back and was still standing over the table, Katie looked up at him and said, "I'm sooo hungry."

And he remembered the sheep from his vision earlier in the day, "The hungry sheep look, and are not fed."

It stopped him. Katie was spiritually hungry. And she wasn't being fed. That's what was really going on here. And if he had a responsibility to nourish the congregation he was about to lead in worship on Sundays, how much more of a responsibility should he have for his own wife-to-be.

Slowly, he sat down in his chair opposite the table from Katie. He was so distracted by his thoughts that he almost missed the chair. He had to catch himself.

"You ok," Katie asked. She reached her hand across the table. He took it. He smiled.

"Yeah. I'm good."

During lunch, he texted Giddy and asked if he could come over and hang out. Giddy lived in an A-frame house down by the lake past Swagler's Farm. He owned his own tree service business and was able to save up enough money to move out of his parents' house about a year ago. There was a pole barn at the end of his driveway near the road where he kept all his tree equipment. His uncle had run a tree business for twenty years, but some unfortunate DUI's had led to brief stint in jail, and he lost his business. He also couldn't get another loan from the bank, so the whole tree business is in Giddy's name. He gives his uncle 50% of the income. He handles all the scheduling and bookkeeping and communication with clients, and Uncle Hank climbs up into the trees with a chainsaw.

Gid also had some free-range chickens in his yard that could go all the way down to the lake and dip their toes in if they wanted to, but they never did. There was an old shed on the property that he made into a coop, and he picked fresh eggs every morning. He also had a few bee boxes in a grove of pine trees along his gravel driveway. He always wanted a bee farm, because he thought it would be cool, but it wasn't going well. He had no idea what he was doing. But he kept his beekeeping suit on the coat rack just inside his door—like a superhero suit, so everybody who entered his house knew right away just how cool he was.

Dave didn't think he was cool when he saw the bee suit. Giddy gave him a quick tour: the wood-burning stove, the huge stainless steel fridge with a quarter of a cow, Giddy bought at Sumner's Farm, stuffed in the freezer. He took him out to see the big wooden deck that looked out over the lake. The sun skated over ripples in the water. Then, he took him up the spiral staircase to the bedroom. The bed was a just a king-sized mattress on the floor. Dave had to duck because the ceiling was so low and the wall sloped. There were porthole windows on both sides of the room that had stunning views.

"This is where I choke the chicken," Giddy told him with a grin. "You know. Shake hands with the milkman." Dave cringed and looked around the room at the posters of half-naked women. He went immediately back down the spiral staircase. Next, Giddy took him down to the basement, which is where he spent most of his time. He had a nice couch down there and a big-screen, plasma tv. The Steelers game was on. Everybody in Picture Creek loved the Steelers even though, they lived closer to Buffalo than they did to Pittsburgh. Honestly, it was probably because, for whatever reason that such things are decided, their local tv station got Steelers games nearly every Sunday.

Anyway, there was a gym in the basement. Giddy had a weight bench down there, a universal machine, a bunch of dumbbells, a pull-up bar mounted to the wall, and a handful of other equipment. There was also a treadmill. Giddy shocked himself twice trying to run a new line from the fuse box so it could have a dedicated outlet. Otherwise, the treadmill tripped the electricity in his whole house as soon as he turned it on.

Dave took off his button-down church shirt and tossed it on the couch. He had on a t-shirt that said, "Jesus Rocks" with a drawing of Jesus with an electric guitar. Dave and Gid started working out and watching the Steelers game—something they used to do together every Sunday when they were in high school. The Steelers were having a decent year and were on the bubble to make the playoffs. Dave had loosely followed the season, mostly just to keep track of his fantasy football team, which had just squeaked into the playoffs. Anyway, he knew enough about the Steelers' season to know that this was a crucial game for them against the Bengals.

Giddy was really throwing some weight around, but Dave's heart wasn't quite into it. Finally, he threw his dumbbells on the floor and said, "Katie's deconstructing."

"Whoa . . . you gotta drop that bee-yotch, bro," Giddy told him. "I'm serious. You don't mess around with that."

"But it's Katie."

"I don't care, bro. I don't care if she's Mother Theresa. Bible tells us not to be unequally yolked. You drop her asset like a slick, wet dookie or a 10-pound kettle bell and pack up your shingles and go home, brother. For real."

Dave shook his head. He had forgotten about Giddy's fake cursing. Gid believed that actually cursing is unbiblical and offensive to God, so he just replaces curse words with other similar-sounding words. He started out in Junior High with insect names. He would say things like, "What the bees?" Or "Holy crickets!" He had gotten slightly more sophistocated with it over the years.

Dave couldn't help but laugh. Then, he eased down on the couch and said, "I don't know, Gid. It ain't that easy. It's not being unequally yolked. It's Katie. She grew up in the church just like me. She knows the Bible just as good as me. She loves the Lord just as much as me."

"Does she believe in the resurrection?"

Dave shrugged. "Yeah. Of couse she does." He shrugged again. "I think."

"Brother. You gotta know that you know that you know. For real, bro. You can't play around with this shalloon. You gotta get out."

Dave laughed. "Shalloon? What the hell's that?"

Gid smiled. "It's a type of wool, dude. They used to use it to line jackets. It's kind of a lighter material. Don't you know anything about fashion," he said matter-of-factly. He racked his weights and grabbed his water bottle. It was filled with a chocolate protein shake. He held it at waist level and shook it for a long, long. . .long time with a very straight face while gazing intently into Dave's eyes.

"What're you doing," Dave asked. "Why're you looking at me like that? . . . What're you doing? . . . Stop it."

And Gid just kept on doing. He never blinked. He never looked away. He never stopped shaking the bottle. Eventually, Dave stopped talking, and they just stood there frozen like that for nearly a minute.

Finally, out of sheer awkwardness, they both burst out laughing at the same time.

"Hey, listen," Gid said slapping his hand on Dave's shoulder. "If you're not gonna dump her, then you gotta ask her the hard questions. You can't just assume it's all gonna work out. You guys have to be on the same page. Seriously. How're you gonna do ministry together if you guys don't believe the same things? How're you gonna raise all your beautiful, annoying kids together? It's gonna be impossible, bro. I'm telling you."

"I don't know, man," Dave said. "I realized today she's going through something really big and heavy and, like, life-changing. You know? And she's kind of doing it alone. She can't really talk to her parents about it. I don't really think there's too many people she can actually open up to and be real with about this. More than anything, right now, she needs to feel supported . . . and loved and cared about. And I think I can give that to her. As her husband."

"Ain't no husband yet."

"No, but it's just a technicality, really. In ancient Israelite culture, you were man and wife the moment you were betrothed. Married. Engaged. They were the same thing."

"Well . . ." Gid shook his head. "But they also ate unleavened bread and stoned people to death."

His voice trailed off as he glanced over Dave's shoulder to catch a glimpse of the Steelers game on the plasma.

"Check it out, man," he said. "Third and six."

Just then, Dave's phone vibrated in his pocket. He whipped it out and punched in his code. It was Katie.

"Is that her," Gid asked. "It's her. I can see it in your face." The vein in his neck started bulging. "Lemme talk to her. Come on. I'll break up with her for ya. Gimme the phone."

"Shut up," Dave waved him away and turned his back. He answered the call and climbed up the spiral staircase for some privacy.

"Hey, babe!"

"Hi," she said brightly on the other end of the phone. He could see her smile in his mind. "Hey, we still good to pick out the trees tomorrow at Candell's?"

Candell's Tree Farm was in Bear Hollow about ten minutes or so away from Picture Creek. Since they were getting married in December, they had naturally decided on a Christmas-themed wedding, so they needed six trees they could decorate and put up at the church and at the lodge where they were holding the reception. Both venues already had Christmas trees up, but they wanted more. More Christmas! They both loved Christmas. It was their favorite holiday.

Also, Dave proposed on Christmas Eve the year before. Dave and Katie had his parent's house all to themselves that whole day as his family was away at his Uncle Pete and Aunt Kathy's house in Pittsburgh. Katie came over in the morning, and Dave made her a big breakfast with eggs and oatmeal. Then, they went sled riding at Swagler's farm. After getting cleaned up, they went to lunch at Chatterly's. Then, they hung together for a few hours watching movies on the couch. Finally, before the sun went down, he took her out into the woods behind his parent's house to their favorite tree. It was a big Fir tree in the middle of an open field. Dave had several long extension cords from the garage, and they strung lights on the old tree and decorated it with his grandmother's vintage bulbs that he and his mom had found in the attic a few weeks earlier. Hidden within the box of Christmas bulbs was the engagement ring. When Katie found it, Dave got down on one knee in the snow and popped the question. She said yes, and they went back in the house to get warm. He made grilled cheese for dinner and then they kissed for eighteen minutes in the light on the front porch. Then, Katie went home and started planning their wedding.

So anyway, now, they needed some Christmas trees for the wedding. So they were going to planning to head over to Candell's tomorrow morning.

"Yeah. That's fine," Dave told her.

"Is everything ok?"

"Oh. Yeah. Yeah. I'm just over at Gid's house. Gimme a second." He breathed out slowly as he finished climbing up the stairs to the first floor. He dropped himself down in Giddy's couch. "Ok. Yeah. I think Candell's sounds awesome! Looking forward to it."

"Ok. Can you pick me up in the morning?"

"Sure. Wanna go out for breakfast?"

"Maybe."

"Hey," he said. "Why couldn't the bicycle make it up the hill?"

"I don't know."

"Because it was two tired."

She laughed faintly. Dave knew, though, that she appreciated his bad jokes. He had a library of really stupid jokes in his brain, and he would bust one out to break tension or lighten the mood.

"How're you feeling," he asked her.

"Ok. I'm a little stressed."

"What? Why? It's not like there's anything important happening this week."

She made a little laughing sound.

"Hey. It's all gonna be alright," he reassured her. "We're gonna be alright."

"Do you think so?"

"Yeah. Of course. I love you, squirrel butt."

"I love you too, babe. . .I'm sorry I didn't tell you sooner about what I've been going through lately."

"It's ok."

"No, I should've told you way sooner. I just. . .there never really seemed like a right time. I didn't wanna tell you over the phone, because I wanted to look you in the eyes. And I wanted to be able to touch you. And we were just apart for so long recently. And before that even when we were together, we were so busy."

She was holding back tears. Dave could feel it. He could hear it in her voice. And then, he heard it when they starting pouring out.

"And I was scared, because I didn't know. . ." she continued, ". . .what you would think of me. And I wanna be a good wife to you. And I wanna make you happy. And I just care so much about what you think of me. And I don't want you to be disappointed in me. I don't want you to think less of me."

"Katie. I love you! I love you. I love you. You are an amazing child of God! You are smart and brave and beautiful! I could never think any less of you or love you any less. I am so proud of you." He was starting to tear up now. "You are doing a really brave thing. And I'm really glad you told me."

"You are?"

"Yeah. We need to be open and honest with each other. We need to share our hurts and our struggles with each other. We need to trust each other with the hard things."

"You're right. I know you're right."

"I am always gonna love you from deep in my heart and deep in my soul. And nothing is ever gonna change that."

"Ok. . .ok," she said through her tears. "I love you too."

"I'll pick you up tomorrow at 8, and we'll go have breakfast."

"Ok."

"And then we'll go cut down trees."

"Ok."

"I love you, Baby!"

"I love you too."

"See you in the morning."

"Bye."

When he left Giddy's house, the sun was setting, and he could see it blazing like a painting over the trees and rippling across the lake like fire. And he thought of his favorite Psalm. Psalm 19.

> "In the heavens God has pitched a tent for the sun.
> ⁵ It is like a bridegroom coming out of the bridal chamber,
> like a champion rejoicing to run his course.
> ⁶ It rises at one end of the heavens
> and makes its circuit to the other;
> nothing is deprived of its warmth."

It speaks of the love God has for us, that He would create such a thing for us. And the love that we can have for each other. A love that reflects the Father's love for us. And what more to life could there possibly be than feeling the warmth of God's love and to rejoice in shining the light of that love onto others?

Katie spilled out onto her mattress. Her hair hung down off the bed in thick, tired curls. She was exhausted, but what relief she felt at David's words to her. Like a tremendous burden lifted off her shoulders. Her cheeks were wet with tears, and she wiped them slowly on her sheets. She drew out a long, slow breath. One she had been holding in for months. And her chest felt lighter.

After a minute, she got up. She grabbed a laundry basket and headed down to the basement. She had held off cleaning her clothes for the last week or so of school so she could do the laundry at home. She liked the peace and quiet of her basement. There was something calming and nourishing about the quiet. In the laundry room in her dorm, it was noisy and crowded and awkward and annoying. But down here, in her parents' basement, she could flick on the space heater, grab a blanket, and curl up on the couch with a good book.

She had A.W. Tozer's Pursuit of God in the basket on top of her dirty shirts. She hadn't read it in over a year. Dave had introduced to the book. He gave it to her randomly on one of his visits to her campus when they were undergrads, and she devoured it all in one night. She had read it four times since then, and she had received more insight from it each time. Her copy was all noted up with Dave's neat comments in the margins and her scribbles and drawings in purple ink all over the pages.

She moved her jeans to the dryer and tossed her shirts in the washer. Then, she dropped herself onto the cozy old, frayed couch and opened to the first page of Tozer's book. She got through about a page and a half before her cell phone rang.

It was a text from Ariel, her friend from Grad School—"Did you tell him yet?"

Katie set the book down and began typing her response, "Yes"

"…And?!?"

"So far it's ok. He's at least trying to be understanding."

"Well he loves you."

"Yes. He does."

"You are SO lucky!"

"I know. But still so much more to talk about. Could go wrong a thousand different ways."

"Hey…you said you were gonna stay positive. Come on, girl!"

"I'm just scared…"

"I told you you need to postpone the wedding. You guys need more time."

"Can't. Too late."

"Not too late to do the right thing."

"And … it's too late for me," Katie typed. "I gotta go to bed."

"You know it, girl! Love you! Sleep tight."

"Good night."

She threw the phone down on the couch cushion. "It's too late," she told the phone.

~

Dave was at home, and everyone else in the house was asleep. Normally, this would be his favorite time of the day, but not tonight. Tonight, he was restless. As a pastor, Dave saw himself as a master of signs. He believes that he has trained himself to see signs in everything. Signs from God. Hidden messages embedded subtly into the world around him. That's what pastors do. They see the spiritual in the mundane. They see the subtext, the slight bend in the meaning of a word. They exegete. They see the signs. So how then could he, a pastor, miss all of Katie's signs? Surely, there had to have been signs. Surely, she had to have left behind small clues of her shifting faith over the past months. . .or maybe years. And surely, he had missed them. Was he so focused on the hidden spiritual signs that he couldn't see the human signs right in front of him? Had he taken Katie for granted? Had he simply been too busy to notice? Or was she so careful not leave behind any discernible signs at all? And if she was so meticulous in submerging every possible sign of her deconversion, what would that mean for their relationship moving forward? She could potentially hide anything at all from him, and he would never be the wiser. He had simply never, ever thought of their relationship in this way before.

He started out in his bedroom trying to listen to a podcast called "The Deconstructionists"—hoping to get some insight into Katie's situation. But he just couldn't do it. He only got six minutes and 38 seconds into the podcast, before he ripped his earbuds out and slammed his cell phone down on the bed. It was just too much. Too much to think about. He needed to not think about it. He needed a distraction.

So he went downstairs to the music room and picked up his acoustic guitar for the first time in he couldn't remember how long. It was a Galilee Guitar, made by a local luthier in his garage about 30 or so miles from Dave's house. A few years ago, he and Katie were driving down Rt.819, a winding mountain road that cuts through what they call the wilds of Pennsylvania, on their way to a wedding in Reading for a couple who had been in their church youth group. They came around a curve on the way down the mountain, and the trees opened up, and the sun poured down on the road. And Dave saw a small handpainted sign nailed to a tree that said, "Galilee Guitars." For some reason that he couldn't explain, he slammed on the brakes and turned down the gravel lane between two rows of walnut trees.

"What're you doing," Katie asked, trying to stay calm.

"I wanna check this place out."

"What place?"

"It's like a guitar shop or something, I think," he told her.

She looked hard at him. "Dave. There's nothing here. . .we're gonna be late for the rehearsal. If we don't die out here first."

But he stayed the course, and eventually they came to a very old, very small house with smoke curling up from the chimney. There was a Jeep Wrangler parked out front. Behind the house was a big mountain lake. And beside the house was a small outbuilding that looked like a garage. Above the garage door was a large, wooden sign with the words "Galilee Guitars" carved intricately across the face of it. At the side of the building, there was a door. Dave pushed it open. He expected a bell ring when he entered, but there was no sound.

Immediately, though, he noticed a strong smell of fresh-cut wood—like pine. There were guitars hanging from the ceiling everywhere—a forest of guitars. Electrics on the left, acoustics on the right.

Dave hadn't written a song in over a year. Maybe he could chronicle this unsettling chapter of his life by writing a song about it. He strummed a few stray chords, but they all felt wrong. Keep it simple, he told himself. And he played a G chord over and over and over, hoping that a melody would shatter out of the chaos of his mind and appear on his lips. But it did not. Suddenly, his fingertips began to feel tingly and numb. And he gently placed his guitar back into its case. He sat for a long time just listening to the tick of the clock and the wind blow against the windows.

Suddenly, he got up quick and walked across the room with purpose. He threw on his Carhartt coat and hat and his red scarf. He pulled on his boots and stepped out into the cold. He felt the cold on his face—almost like a kind of heat at first on his cheeks, but as it moved deeper into his body, he felt the vicious cold of the air. A powerful shiver shook through his whole body. The snow crunched under his boots. He went over to a log pile that his parents kept inside a wooden lean-to between two trees. He lit a fire at their stone firepit. He worked quick and confident with a fierce kind of focus. As a former Royal Ranger, he was a crack firebuilder, and within just a few minutes, the fire was blazing.

He sat back in one of the wooden Adirondack chairs and heaved a sigh. That was the end of his plan. The end of his purpose. He had no more ideas.

So he waited. He leaned back in the chair and put his boots up on top of the fire ring. And he looked up into the vast, dark sky. And he felt alone. Empty. Lost in the wild vastness of time and space. There was no sound anywhere at all. No twigs breaking or dogs barking and car engines running. Just a deep, still silence. The stars broke apart in the sky with a brilliant flash and then quickly collected themselves back together—over and over like a ballet of lights. And then the whole sky started to rotate, and Dave wondered if he was witnessing the turning of the earth. But the sky wasn't turning. It was folding, and all the stars were tumbling like diamonds into one small corner of the sky. And the sky began to rip and tear apart, and the seam broke away right over him like a crack of lightning that struck down into the firepit.

He woke up. The fire was mostly burnt out, but the embers were still hot, and one last tongue of fire whipped and cracked and danced for a second before becoming very still. And then it disappeared.

"You give beauty for ashes." Dave heard the words as if someone had spoken them. He recognized it as a line from Isaiah 61, where the prophet is trying to comfort the mourners. But it was also a line from a song that Dave and Katie sang together a few times at church with the worship team when they were both home for summer break—"Graves Into Gardens" by Elevation Worship and Brandon Lake.

He sprang up out of the Adirondack chair and took off into the woods. He crossed over Picture Creek at the bridge his family had put in years ago and went to the Christmas tree he and Katie had decorated last Christmas on the night he proposed. The lights were still strung, but they weren't plugged in.

As his eyes adjusted in the dark, he noticed something strange. The tree was split down the middle and the two halves were bending in opposite directions. He could see where it had been struck by lightning. He put his finger in the crack and felt the bark of the tree where it was healing. The young bark was slick and smooth under his fingers.

"She struck us with lightning," he said out loud to the tree. "But I think we can heal." This was perhaps the sign he had been hoping for.

Chapter 3

Monday

KATIE WOKE THE NEXT morning feeling unsettled. It surprised her, because she had felt so good about things when she fell asleep last night. She pulled the blankets over her head and decided that there's just something unsettling about waking up. It just takes a while to really settle into the day, at least that's what she was telling herself.

She forced herself to break out from under the blankets. It was cold in her room. In winter, she always slept in layers of warm clothes and thick, wool knee socks (her favorites were the ones her Mom made for her when she was a kid), because her room stayed so tragically cold. She stood up and worked to keep her eyes open. She creaked slowly down the steps, and each step felt a little bit warmer. Her dad was eating a bowl of cereal on the living room couch. When she was halfway down the steps, she could hear his spoon tapping against the bowl. And then she heard the creak of her mom's rocking chair against the hardwood floors.

Creak. Craack. Ting ting ting. Creak. Craack. Ting ting ting.

She stopped. The sounds continued with that same rhythm. She reached out to touch the herringbone patterned wallpaper that slanted up the walls in the stairwell to her bedroom. It had been forever since she had noticed it. It had long become just part of the background of her life. It was a faded red color. Must have faded over time, she thought, but she honestly didn't remember it looking any different. When her fingers finally brushed against the wallpaper, she fell into a dream, for a split second, where all of the moments she spent in this stairwell through her whole life rushed through her mind and then stopped and settled on one moment when she was 14. She was running up the steps to her room, and Dave was chasing after her. That night, they had sat on her bed and talked for over an hour. And then he kissed her. That was their first kiss.

"Morning, Kit," her Dad interrupted her dream from the bottom of the stairwell. "You want some Lucky Charms?" For as long as she could remember, his nickname for her had been Kit.

"No thanks, Dad."

"You ok?"

"Yeah. I'm going out for breakfast with Dave."

"Ok, Sweetie. Have a good time."

~

Dave woke up with a song in his heart. He brushed his teeth and took a shower. He threw on some jeans and a gray sweater. Singing the whole time. When he picked up his phone to check the time, he heard his Mom start playing her fiddle in the music room, which meant only one thing—it was time for Family Band.

Dave crashed down the steps. The music room was long and narrow with a big, bright window. When he got there, his Mom was wailing away on the fiddle, and his Dad was plucking the upright bass. He grabbed an Alvarez acoustic from a guitar stand and sat in a metal folding chair. His fingers began playing notes before he even had time to think. His foot was tapping. His head was bobbing. Before long, his brothers had joined them. Luke was smacking the drum kit, and Jonah played keys on the old, Steinway acoustic upright piano. They were just jamming. Feeling the notes. Feeling each other.

When Dave took his turn to solo, he surprised everyone by slowing everything down and even shifting into a different time signature. Quickly, everyone settled into time with him, like when a dead tree branch falls into a stream and the water splashes for a moment but quickly diverts and sets a new course. He gazed out the picture window where thin, spiring icicles tricked the sunlight in a thousand different ways at once. And the white-tipped branches of the fir trees shook in the wind and spun the snow in gentle, gleaming threads all over the sky. The firs in the backyard bent and shook and rolled along the foothills, blurring to gray on a bending horizon.

~

Katie got ready for the day on autopilot. She wasn't really thinking about anything, but she wasn't not thinking either. She just floated through the house, doing what she needed to do. When she was finally ready for the day, she slid open the door to the sun room and stepped out onto the cold carpet. Slowly, she slid down into a faux-leather couch and scanned her eyes over the plants along the wall of windows. Her Mom grew plants out here all year long. It was cold, but she had a little gas heater that kept the temperature at about 40 degrees. Katie blinked at the viny plants that lined the room in window boxes.

There was a Christmas tree by the door, covered with quirky orna-ments her mom had handmade over the years. Katie remembered helping her to make a few of them back in the day. Her eyes moved to the window and the sun peeking over the trees.

That's when she noticed a ghost reflecting in the window, coming closer. And she felt her father's hand grip her shoulder.

"Oh gracious Heavenly Father," he began. "Lord God please be with my Katie. You are the Prince of Peace. Give her your peace today. A peace that surpasses all understanding. You are the Author of hope. Breathe your hope into her heart, Father. You are the Waymaker, and I pray that you make straight a path for Katie. Light up a way for her in the darkness. You are the Creator, God. You are our Lord. We praise you. We magnify your name. For there is no one greater. Humbly, we ask this in Thy name. Amen."

Katie looked up at her Dad. He was smiling down at her.

"Thanks, Dad."

He walked around in front of her and sat next to her on the couch. "It's cold out here, Kit. What're you doing out here?"

She shrugged. "Just came out to think, I guess."

"Everything ok?"

"Yeah. It's fine."

"Got a lot on your mind. This is a weighty time in your life. I get it. This is one of the most important weeks of your life in some ways. You know, I don't think I've ever told anyone this before but two days before your mother and I got married, I threw up. I was still livin' with your Papaw and Mamaw back then. I lived in a room above their garage. I was up all night. Couldn't sleep a wink. I just tossed and turned and tossed and turned. I was like good night. What is wrong with me? And then I just started feeling tense all over. Like. Like I don't know like what. Like the moment you slam on the brakes so you don't run over a deer. And I jumped out of bed and ran to the bathroom and barfed right there in the sink."

"Well that's a disgusting story."

"The big moments in your life. You think you expect they'll be filled with joy. That you'll feel a certain way. But when you're actually in the middle of it, it doesn't quite feel like you thought it would. And that can be scary. But it's perfectly normal. And . . ." he tapped his knuckles gently against her jeans. "Dave is a truly good man. He can make you a great life. You can have a great life together. I believe that in my bones. You too are made for each other. And I see the love you guys share. I have eyes. He adores you, Kit."

"I know he does," she said. She pulled the sleeves of her sweater down over her hands and started picking at the threads. "But do you think I'm good for him." She was looking down at her sweater hands.

"What?" Her dad leaned forward and placed his hand gently on her back. "Of course you are, Love." He slid closed to her. "Look at me," he told her.

She slowly turned her wet eyes toward him.

"You are lovely and amazing and beautiful inside and out. You're a shining angel! You are God's gift to the world. And you're God's gift to Dave too."

He hugged her. She put her hand up under his arm and laid it on his back.

"Thanks, Daddy."

"I love you, Sweetheart."

"Love you too."

～

The sun was shining. Dave was driving. He had the radio cranked up. Listening to Graves Into Gardens. Bum-bum-bum-BUM! He was playing air drums on the steering wheel when he turned onto Katie's road. He was feeling good. He was gonna love Katie forever. They were gonna have kids and grow old together and sit side by side holding hands in matching rocking chairs until they die and go to Heaven and live forever as man and wife, praising God into eternity.

He pulled into her driveway and pulled up behind her dad's Jetta. He got out of the car. Since he was parked on a hill, the car door swung closed on its own. He bounded up the walkway and leapt to the top of her porch steps with a song in his heart.

Bing bong. He rang the doorbell. His foot was tapping. The snow crackled on the porch. Bing bong.

The door swung open. He felt a gust of warmth from inside the house. Then, quickly, the cold overcame it.

She was there in the doorway. She looked sad. Her body seemed small and tired. Her eyes were just vessels like blue glass vases with nothing in them. For a moment, it took his breath away. He opened his mouth to speak, but he had no breath to form any words. Slowly, his shoulders drooped.

"How's it going," he finally asked her.

"Fine."

He knew when Katie said she was fine that she wasn't fine. "You have breakfast?" He reached out for her hand, but he somehow ended up grabbing her elbow in an awkward effort to lead her out of the house. Despite the awkwardness, she followed his lead and closed the door behind her.

"No," she said as they walked down the steps together in the snow.

"Wanna go to Galiffa's?" Galiffa's was a smart casual restaurant and bakery in Bear Hollow that was known for its spectacular but extravagantly-priced Sunday brunch. But they were open five times a week for breakfast, and their weekday menu was more reasonably priced. It was set in an upcycled horse barn.

Katie shrugged. "Sure."

Dave was about to speak when he slipped on a large patch of ice on the walkway. His leg went flying out in front of himself like he was punting a football, but he managed to catch his footing quickly. His heart was beating fast. Light struck off an icicle that twisted down from the downspout. He heard ice crackling in the gutters.

He was ok. He turned his attention to her. He held the car door open for her and ran around to the driver's side. He was disheartened by her sadness, but he could feel glimmers of hope, and he was determined to brighten her mood.

When he got in the car, he pulled his phone out of his coat pocket and opened the playlist he had made that morning. He knew Katie couldn't resist Christmas Carols. She absolutely loved them, sang them all year long. He started with the Pentatonix version of Silent Night, which was one of her favorites.

They drove for several minutes in silence. Katie was enjoying the music and the snowy landscape out her car window. She felt warm and comfortable in his car. But deeper than that was a feeling of unease.

Dave leaned forward and pushed a button on his phone to change the song. Katie looked away. Everywhere she looked, there was snow. The new song started, and she recognized it right away.

"I searched the world, but it couldn't fill me," Brandon Lake sang out of the car stereo. "Man's empty praise and treasures that fade are never enough."

"You remember this song," Dave asked her.

She nodded.

"Remember when we went on that retreat last summer at some camp, like, out in the woods? And the worship band played this song and absolutely killed it?"

She leaned forward in her seat. She looked over into his eyes, and he looked just like a little kid. He was so excited to share this song with her. Graves into Gardens—that was the name of it. She blinked at Dave, and he was looking back at the road.

"Nothing is better than You," he sang at the top of his lungs.

She couldn't help but smile at him. What a goofball, she thought. He was drumming on the steering wheel and on the dashboard. And by the time the bridge arrived, she was ready to belt it out. "You turn mourning to dancing! BUM BUM BUM BUM! You give beauty for ashes! BUM BUM BUM BUM!" On the bum bum bum bums, she pounded her fists against the dashboard and flung her hair back and forth and stomped her foot on the floor mat. She felt the weight of everything shaking off of her body like water. She felt the tension in her shoulders dissolve away. For a moment, she felt nothing but love, and she knew it was the Holy Spirit.

Dave gazed over at her in the passenger seat and fell in love with her all over again. He saw sunlight flash in her like pops of electricity. He watched her body move free and beautiful. He wanted to kiss her, but he didn't want her to stop. He didn't want to take his eyes off of her for one second.

They pulled into Galiffa's. From the road, it was about a half mile drive on a snow-covered, gravel driveway through the farm. The parking lot, which was really just a big field, was packed.

"You ever been here before," Katie asked.

"Yeah. Once. We came here once a long time ago for Mom's Birthday. I was a kid, but I remember the food was amazing, and they had a live band with a fiddle player. And the ceilings were like crazy high. But I just couldn't believe the food! Omelettes and bacon and sausage and fresh fruits and pancakes with real maple syrup. It was like one of those feasts in the Bible where the king invites all his friends and they eat, like, all the best food in the whole kingdom. It was incredible."

"What feast in the Bible?"

"You know." He raised one hand and made a confusing gesture. "The mene mene tekel upharsin feast in Babylon with the writing on the wall."

She looked blankly at him.

"You know what I'm talking about," he countered.

She smiled at him. "Actually, I don't have any idea." They both laughed a little at that, and Dave held the door open for her.

They had a 15-minute wait, so they found a seat on a bench in an old horse stall that had been decorated for Christmas with lights and wreaths and garlands. There was a Christmas tree in the far corner with a small train set around it.

"This is place is fancy," she told him.

"But also rustic."

"I guess so."

They sat on the bench with their knees touching.

Dave looked over at her. He laid his hand gently into hers, and their fingers weaved together.

"So, babe, let me ask you," he began.

"Yeah."

"What is it that got you thinking in this way? That caused you start doubting things?"

Her jaw started pulsing as if she was chewing gum. "Uh. I don't know. I guess . . . I guess maybe it started with your Mom. I remember in high school, watching your Mom up in front of the Sanctuary, leading worship like a boss and never getting the recognition she deserved. I think that's maybe the first time I ever felt, like, I don't know, like, the church has problems. The church actually has the capacity to hurt people."

"Yeah. Of course it does. None of us is perfect. We're all sinners."

"But I think there's something fundamentally flawed about the church today in our time, and the way they live out the Gospel. There's something about it that's just not right."

"Yeah. I think that just comes back to people being flawed. You're never gonna find a perfect church, because the church is made up of the people. And people are flawed."

"God made us to be flawed?"

He shrugged. "We're flawed because of our choices."

"Well, you can't have it both ways. If people are good. If God made people to be good then we would make good choices. If we make bad choices, then we're not good. If we make bad choices, then God didn't make us good."

"You know what I mean, though. It's the Fall. Not our choices. Adam and Eve's choices that make us flawed. You know, the Fall broke something in Creation. And now it's flawed. We're flawed because of it. God created everything and He saw that it was good. And He gave humans free will. And they chose to follow their own way instead of God's way. The same choice any of us would make at some point. And now, we're cursed. Our institutions, our political systems, our societies, even our churches are corrupted by it."

"But how can you say that God made us good if we'll always make the wrong choice, if we're always gonna choose our own way?"

"Because that's what free will is. God loved us enough to give us free will, to choose our own way. If He created us to always choose His way, then we'd be like robots. We wouldn't be free at all."

"But if God was all-powerful and all-knowing and all that, why would He ever create humans in the first place if He knew from the very beginning that they were gonna mess it all up. And cause millenia of pain and heartache and suffering. Cancer and hurricanes and war and violence. Why would He do that?"

"Because He loves us."

"How can say that?" Her voice was rising. "How can you say that when He had to've known that He would be creating all this suffering and pain."

"Because there's beauty too. The world isn't all pain and suffering. You're making it sound like life is constant torment. Like we're in Hell already. Life is beautiful and amazing. I mean, come on, every single breath you take is a complete, freakin' miracle. And here we are, these lowly creatures, these tiny little specks of dust in the universe, and each and every one of us gets the chance to have a personal and life-altering relationship with the Creator of the sun and the moon and stars and all the galaxies in the whole universe."

Katie was shaking her head. "I don't know. I can't see it. What about the people, the little orphaned kids living on trash heaps in Haiti surviving off scraps of trash every day of their entire, miserable existence. And then they die."

"You are just a barrel of monkeys today," he smiled at her. That was a phrase his mother used to use all the time when he was growing up. "I think that's why it's so important that we become the hands and feet of Christ in this world. God isn't gonna come down outta the sky and fix all the problems. He's calling us to go out into the world and serve."

"But why doesn't God fix everything? If He's really all-powerful and all-loving, then He should make a better way."

He pulled his hand away and sat forward with his hands on his knees. "I don't understand this," he said through his teeth. "Yes. There's bad things in the world, but there's also beauty. I mean even just the fact that you and I were ever even born is a freakin' miracle. Every little detail in the history of the entire universe had to go exactly like it did or else we might not even exist. I heard recently that if the strength of gravity was just slightly, just a fraction different than what it is, higher or lower, then planets may have never even formed and life would have never existed."

"What does that have to do with anything?'

"I'm saying." He turned toward her. "I'm just saying there's 9 billion people in the world. How many of them do you think are so miserable on planet earth that they genuinely wish they'd never been born?"

"Ten percent."

"Are you kidding me?! Ten percent? That's crazy! There's absolutely no way. You're saying if there was a 100 people in this restaurant right now, ten of them are so beaten down by life that they would prefer they had never even existed. Never saw a sunrise. Never smelled fresh-baked bread. Never ate pizza. That's really what you think?"

She shrugged. "I don't know. People are hurting, David."

"I think out of 100 people, it's unlikely that a single person would wish they had never been born."

"Then, I think you haven't seen enough of the world."

Dave looked down and rolled his eyes so Katie couldn't see it. He wanted to say, "And how much of the world have you seen?" But he didn't. It felt like too mean of a thing to say. He looked down at his hands. They were both palms up in his lap. He was surprised to see that his body was positioned in such a way. It seemed to him a completely ridiculous way to be sitting. He couldn't imagine why he would be sitting this way.

"Ecchols."

Dave and Katie both looked up. There was a young woman looking at them. She had her hair pinned up, and she was carrying two menus across her chest. She led them to their table. It was in the corner near the bathrooms. They both took their coats off and hung them on the backs of their chairs. Dave took off his knit cap and shoved it into his coat pocket. They both sat down and slid their legs under the table.

They scanned their menus for a few minutes.

"Everything looks so good," David said. "What're you gonna get?"

"Um . . . I don't know. It's all so expensive."

Dave looked up at her and reached across the table to lay his hand on hers. "It's ok, baby. I got it."

"Well, yeah . . . obviously," she said with a grin. "Maybe I'll get a cheesy bacon omelette."

"Sounds good."

"What about you? What're you getting?"

"Chocolate chip pancakes and a side of bacon. Did I mention they have real maple syrup here?"

"You did, yeah."

"You just can't get that anywhere."

"You know I thought of something else. Something much earlier, where my faith started kind of changing."

"Ok . . ."

"You remember Miss Bowhuckey?"

"Miss Bowhuckey? No . . . wait. Oh. The Sunday school teacher. Like first grade. Maybe second grade?"

"Yeah. Well, I remember feeling like I couldn't ask questions in that class."

"Why?"

"Remember? You asked her why the snake in the Garden of Eden could talk. 'Snakes don't talk,' you said. And she made it seem like you just tossed your cookies on her shoes."

He laughed.

"That kind of thing used to happen all the time in church. Not just Miss Bowhuckey. They all did that. None of those Sunday School teachers wanted us to ask questions. To question the Bible. To question their beliefs.

I think they were scared. Scared of our questions. And I think I just eventually learned to stop questioning. And then over time, I started to feel stuck. You know? Kind of trapped. A little lost."

He blinked at her and nodded. He had some sense of what she was talking about, but mostly, he didn't. The waiter came, and they ordered. They each took a big long drink of water, almost at the same time.

When he put his glass back down on the table, he said, "I think I know what you mean."

"If we have kids, I don't think I want to send them to Sunday School. Because for me, it affected me. Even in school, I wouldn't ask questions. I never asked questions. Not to my parents. I just kept it all in. I was afraid."

"Well, I don't agree with that. I mean, we as parents have to create an environment where our kids feel safe to ask questions. Where it's normal to ask questions. Where their questions are respected and encouraged. Look. We don't want Miss Bowhuckey answering those hard questions. We don't. She shouldn't be answering them. That's our job. That's an opportunity for us breathe into our kids what we believe and what we hope for them in their lives. Or to be humble and honest and to admit when we don't really have an answer. That's not for the Sunday School teacher to steal from us."

"But they shouldn't make kids feel less than just for having questions."

"No. Of course not. But we can't control that."

"We can. We can control it. We can *not* send them to Sunday School."

"But look at the good things that can come from Sunday School too. They learn to value Bible stories. Many of the things we value in our home are reinforced. They learn to respect and treasure the Bible and their faith. They make friends with kids from good families who value many of the same things we do."

"They learn Bible stories where a whale eats a man and then pukes him up on a beach. And where God destroys the whole world and the entire human race with a flood. Just murders everybody. Just what they're teaching to six-year-olds."

"Why are you always so focused on the negative?"

"Why is there so much negativity in the church?"

"Because the world isn't perfect. We can't spend our lives wrapped up in our own little cocoon. Kids have to learn to fight. To be strong. To stand up for what's right. Or this world will tear them down. And they need to know they serve a God who will fight for them."

"He'll fight for them if they obey Him. And if they don't, He'll wipe them off the face of the Earth."

"Is that really what you think the Bible says?"

"No. But I do think that's what kids learn from those stories when they're not allowed to ask questions."

"I don't know, babe. I think the Bible is the source of all wisdom and the foundation of an abundant life. And I think our children should be taught to honor it and respect it and value it. And sending kids to Sunday School can help achieve that."

She shrugged.

"And I thought that's what you wanted to. I thought we were on the same page on this."

After a few awkward minutes of silence passed, their waiter brought their food. And they ate.

"This is absolutely delicious," she told him while devouring her first bite. "How's your real maple syrup."

"It's glorious," he said through a mouthful of pancakes. "This is the truth." A small piece of pancake sprayed out of his mouth.

They ate until they were full. Katie looked down at her spoon when she was finished eating her side of fresh strawberries, and she saw her distorted reflection in the curve of the spoon. Her forehead looked outlandishly wide and thin. She laughed for a second. Then, she said. "And I guess the most recent thing that happened that caused me to question the faith I grew up with is . . . I met someone at grad school who was traumatized by the church."

"How so?" He looked up from his plate with nothing left but a puddle of syrup. "What do you mean?"

"The church basically condemned this person. The people from the church said some really nasty things to them and did some disgusting things behind their back. Treated them just awfully. Eventually, the lead pastor of the church and the youth pastor had a meeting with them and effectively threw them out of the church. Asked them to leave and never come back. And then they're parents basically disowned them, because of their religious beliefs. They've been on their own since they were 16. It's really sad."

"Are you talking about more than one person?"

"What do you mean? No. It's just one person."

"Ok. What happened? Why did they ask her to leave?"

"Just for being who they are."

"I don't understand this story. There had to be a reason."

"This person is gender non-binary."

"Oh. I get it now."

"Their name is Ariel."

"Wait. What? Who . . . ?"

"Ariel."

"I know. But you keep saying they. And this is one person?"

"David. Stop being an idiot. It's the 21st century. Their pronoun is they."

Dave shook his head with a quick snap. His mind was in the process of being blown. "Is Ariel her real name?" It was the only question he could think to ask.

"It's the name they've chosen."

"Why did they change her name?"

"Their old name didn't suit them anymore."

"Ok." He swallowed. His mind was lost in a fog, and he had taken a wrong turn somewhere. "How well do you know this person?"

"Very well. We're very close."

"How close?"

"We talk on the phone almost every day."

"Why haven't I met her . . . they?"

"Because I was afraid how you would respond and what you might think of them. And of me."

He blinked. Then, he shrugged. "I'd love to meet her. If she means a lot to you then I would be honored to meet her."

"They'll be at the wedding."

"That's great!"

"I'm really nervous about it. I just don't know how people are going to respond."

"When you say gender nonbinary, what exactly does that mean?"

"Um . . . it means they don't identify as a man or a woman."

"Well . . . I guess. I know basically what it means. I guess I want to know what it means for this particular person. Does she wear boy's clothes? Does she like to play sports . . . or . . . I don't know. Does she like to hunt or something? What is it about being a woman that she doesn't identify with?"

"Well they're not a woman."

"Right. But you know what I mean. What . . . How does . . . this person know that . . . they . . . is . . . are . . . is not a woman?"

"They just know. It's all about how they feel."

"I understand that, but there has to be a reason why she would feel so strongly. Like, I put my identity in Christ. Because I believe. But I believe, because of reasons. Some people might disagree with my reasons, but I have my reasons that seem right to me, and I've chosen to live by them. But I can't live my life based just on feelings with no reason. I wouldn't be able to function."

"I'm sure if you asked them, they would have reasons."

"I guess so. But what do you think they could be? I'd love to talk about that with them when I meet her. . .them."

"Ariel's not a she. When you meet them, you have to respect their pronouns. It would be very hurtful."

"Is he a dude?"

"What?"

"Is Ariel a dude?"

"Ariel doesn't identify. . ."

"Katie! Is Ariel a biological male?"

"Well, technically yes, but. . ."

"And you talk to him on the phone every day?"

"Yes."

"Katie. He's trying to get in your pants."

"That is not true. You don't know anything, David. That's ridiculous."

"Have you told him about our little conflict here this week leading up to the wedding?"

"Yes."

"Has he tried to get you to call it off?"

"Well. Yes, but. . ."

"Katie! He wants to be with you. He wants me gone."

"That's insane, David! You don't know what you're talking about."

Dave was not at all pleased with the tone this conversation was taking. And he was angry with himself, because of it. He was determined to be supportive, and it was all unraveling.

"I'm sorry, Katie. I don't wanna argue with you. What I want is to be supportive of what you're going through. We're on the same team. We need to uplift each other."

"It's ok to argue and disagree. I think it's good to get things like this out in the open. But you're wrong about Ariel. You don't know anything about my relationship with them. You just have to trust me that there's nothing going on there."

"Of course I trust. Absolutely!"

"Good.

"What are some books you're reading or podcasts you're listening to or whatever that are helping you through this?"

"Um . . . Well, I'm about halfway through The Universal Christ by Richard Rohr. It's AMAZING. It will blow the doors off your brain. It has really opened my mind to understanding Christ differently."

"What's it. Like. What's it about?"

"Uh. It's about seeing Christ in everyone and everything. Seeing Christ in Creation."

"That sounds interesting."

"Yeah. Um. What else? Oh. I'm listening to this podcast called Home-brewed Christianity with Tripp Fuller. I think you might like him. He's really funny. He's into Process Theology. Which, I guess, to think about it in its simplest form is to say that everything is fundamentally a process. Even God is a process. Changing over time."

"OK. . ."

"And I like Thomas Jay Oord. He wrote this book about free will called God Can't. He talks about how evil and suffering exist because of free will. And God loves us so much that He can't limit our free will. It's something He can't do, he chooses not to do, because of His great love for us."

"An interesting thought."

"Oh. Um. . .Rob Bell. He has a podcast I listen to. I just love the way he talks about God and religion."

"I know Rob Bell."

"Yeah?"

"He wrote Love Wins."

"Yes."

"Where he talks about how everyone eventually ends up in Heaven."

"Yes. Basically."

"But then what would be the point of this life?"

"Do you think that this life is nothing but some sort of testing ground for Heaven?"

"I wouldn't put it like that exactly. But I believe, I guess, that this life, this world matters, because it has eternal significance. If we all end up ulti-mately in the same place, then the choices we make on earth don't matter. What we believe doesn't matter."

"It matters to us."

"Ok. Sure."

"It matters to the people around us. The people we love. Why does it need to mean anything more than that?"

"Because it matters to God. The choices we make matter to God. We have to make choices based on what matters to God and not based on what matters to the people around us. And I think that's exactly what Rob Bell was doing when he wrote Love Wins. He was more concerned about his audience, his followers, than he is concerned about God. He wants people to like him. He wants people to think he's so smart and so moral and so good. He cares more about that than following God's commands."

"How could you possibly know that? You don't know that. You're mak-ing it up."

"Of course I don't know it. That's just what I think. He just seems phony to me. I watched a video interview with him once, and I just didn't trust a single thing he said. He seemed too stilted."

She shrugged. "Ok."

"And I just think all that universalism stuff is so un-Biblical. I think the Bible makes it pretty clear that some people are going to Heaven and others to Hell. I think 1 Corinthians 6 says it pretty clearly. But It's not for us judge. We don't know. We can't know who is gonna go where or why. We just gotta have faith that Jesus died to cover our sins."

"But don't you think Jesus died for the whole world? For ALL people?"

"Of course!"

Katie was about to say something. It was on the tip of her tongue. She could feel the words crackling on her lips and bubbling up in the back her throat. She didn't quite know what the words were going to be, but she knew the feeling. It was going to be harsh. Mean-spirited. Laced with poi-son, burning on her tongue. She made a confused gesture with her hand. And then she swallowed it all back. All the poison words. All the crackling, hurtful feelings. All the stinging thoughts and intentions. She swallowed them back into herself, into her inner workings, and she felt the gears inside of her sticking and straining against it. A pocket of empty air popped sud-denly into her mouth, and she coughed it out violently. It made her whole body heave. She shook and tremble at the force of it. Her eyes were wet. He cheeks slick with tears. She was doubled over with her head between her knees. But only for a moment. Suddenly, it stopped. And it was over.

Dave jumped and crossed the table, silverware clanging. "You ok?" He was beside her in a flash with his hand on her shoulder, then her elbow, then her hand. He was kneeling beside her.

"I'm ok," she said with a voice like a ratchet. "I'm ok."

Her facial expression began to return to normal, so Dave got up and moved slowly back to his seat.

"I thought you might've been choking and a piece of bacon," he said. "Thought I might have to do the heimlech."

"Nah. I'm fine," she croaked. After a moment, her inner gears began to turn again. She could feel them clicking and loosening. But they were charged differently, with a new electric pulse that she felt surging out to her fingertips. "You know," she said, "who else I've been reading?"

He blinked at her.

"Tozer. I'm re-reading The Pursuit of God."

"Really?"

"Yeah."

"Me too! I'm re-reading it!"

"No way. That's awesome! It's such a powerful book. I find it to be just as helpful today as it was when I first read it."

He smiled at her.

"You introduced me to Tozer." She smiled back at him.

"I know. I remember."

For a long moment, they sat together in silence and gazed into each other's eyes. Dave reached across the table, and Katie took his hand. Their fingers rubbed together like sandpaper, they were so chapped and rough from the cold.

"I love you," he told her. "We can work this out." He came over slowly to her side of the table, and they kissed.

Outside, it was warmer than they expected. The sun was shining. They could hear the snow thawing and the icicles crashing down off the gutters.

They got in Dave's car and drove the rest of the way to Candel's Tree Farm. The parking lot was snowy and empty. It was late in the season, and most of their best trees had already been picked. But the farm was open for business. They have a smiley, plywood Santa at the entrance whenever they're open.

Dave and Katie held hands and crunched through the snow. They walked into the sun and marveled at the gentle rolling white hills, speckled with pine trees and spruces and firs. There was a maze of trees leading to their tractor ride. Each tree in the maze was marked with a wooden post that named the species of each different type of tree. Dave and Katie took their gloves off and felt the needles. They smelled the branches and noted the subtle shades of green.

When they got to the start of the tractor ride, there was a big John Deere with a wagon but no driver. So they climbed up into the wagon and waited.

"You mentioned a Bible verse earlier," Katie said. "I think it was 1 Corinthians 6. What is that one?"

"Let's see." Dave pulled out his iPhone. There was no cell reception, but he had the Bible app downloaded onto his phone, so he brought up the passage and read it out loud. "Or do you not know that wrongdoers will not inherit the kingdom of God? Do not be deceived: Neither the sexually immoral nor idolaters nor adulterers nor men who have sex with men."

"Ok."

Dave noted another passage just a few verses later. He read, "The body, however, is not meant for sexual immorality but for the Lord, and the Lord for the body. [14] By his power God raised the Lord from the dead, and he will raise us also. [15] Do you not know that your bodies are members of Christ himself? Shall I then take the members of Christ and unite them with a prostitute? Never!"

Katie sat back against the wooden beams. "What do you think it means to inherit the kingdom of God?"

"I think it means they won't get into Heaven."

"Why do you think that?"

"That's a very common interpretation of the phrase."

"But why wouldn't it just say Heaven if that's actually what it meant?"

"Well . . . back then heaven just meant, like, the sky," he explained. "The Apostle Paul and the writers of the New Testament were just trying to put words to an idea that didn't really have words for it yet."

"Do you think that's right? Don't you think he was talking about the Kingdom of God here on Earth rather than in Heaven?"

"Well . . . I don't know. Why would you think that?"

"Doesn't Jesus say multiple times in the Bible that the Kingdom of God is here?"

"Yes. He says the Kingdom of God has arrived. But He could've been talking about Himself. The Divine has arrived on earth. I am here. I am a part of Heaven. I am Heaven on earth."

"I guess maybe it could be." She shrugged. "But it's here. It's not in Heaven. It isn't something to be in the future, like, when we die. It's here now."

He shrugged. "I don't know. I just think He means, I am here now. And I'm bringing the keys to Heaven. I'm opening the door to Heaven for you."

"But don't you see how it simply isn't as clear as you are making it out to be?"

"I don't know, but whatever Kingdom of God means, it certainly means something good. It is something you would want to inherit. Inheriting it would mean that you've found favor with God. And men who have sex with men will never inherit the kingdom of God."

"Do you think a homosexual relationship back then was the same as it is today?"

"Probably not."

"Back then, they were probably more secretive and more like seedy . . . or something. Not like the deep, meaningful relationships that they are today."

"Deep, meaningful relationships?"

"Yeah. Gay men, lesbian women, today they can all have lifelong, single-partner relationships. Like they couldn't back in Biblical times. Paul wasn't exactly talking about the same thing then that we are talking about today."

"So what! If it was wrong back then, why would it be ok today?"

"And does the Bible say anything about women having sex with women?"

"Not that I know of, but Jesus teaches us that life isn't about us pursuing our own desires. It's about living for something greater. That's the Kingdom of God. It's the something greater that can happen when you commit your life to Christ. When you commit to living more like Christ and following His teachings."

"So everybody should just strive to be miserable then?"

"No. Of course not. There's nothing miserable about living an abundant life. About living for God. There's nothing miserable about foregoing immediate pleasures and living for something spiritual, something with deeper meaning. That's actually the opposite of miserable. That's joy."

"I just think that reading the Bible the way you do is causing people to hate the LGBT community, to oppress them and marginalize them. Can't you see that happening in the church?"

"Baby, why would you try and negotiate with the Bible over this? The Bible is . . ."

"Everybody negotiates with the Bible."

"Whaddayou mean?"

"Everybody interprets the Bible according to their own individual biases and preferences and experiences. There is no one right way to interpret all of Scripture. Everybody negotiates with the Bible based on what they already think is true."

"Well no. There's not one right way, but there's . . ."

"I'm trying to get back to what the origin intent was of the writers of the Bible."

"No you're not. You're not!"

"I am!"

"You're talking about how homosexual relationships are different today."

"Only as a way of highlighting that Paul was talking about something different than we are today."

"If you were really trying to get back to the original intent of the authors, then you'd be looking at how the ancient writers interpreted them. We're two thousand years removed. But Augustine was only a few hundred. He was closer in context to the Biblical writers. He understood their original intent better than we ever could, and he condemned homosexuality. You're foolin' yourself, Katie. You're not even doing what you think you're doing. You're following along with these things, because you think they're kind and compassionate things. People are making it seem like it's the kind and compassionate way. But it's not. It's condemning people to hell. It's making people feel comfortable about their sins here on earth and setting them up with an eternal home in hell."

There was a tear rolling down her cheek. "You can't believe," she shouted. "You can't believe that a loving God would send a person to burn for eternity in hell just because of who they love. That is disgusting! No one can actually believe that."

"Ultimately, God will decide who gets into heaven and who goes to hell."

"David, it's this sort of theology that is destroying the church and marginalizing good people who . . ."

"Katie, you keep talking about the church as if it's some monolithic thing. I don't understand what you're saying. People are flawed. Churches are flawed. No one can love like God loves. We all fall short."

"Didn't Tozer say that churches have to strive. Strive to be better, to be more than they can be. That Christians have to strive to be more than humanly possible."

"Yes. But it's only possible with the help of the Holy Spirit."

"Do you think the Holy Spirit is in the church or not?"

"I mean. I don't know. Katie. I guess . . . The Holy Spirit is in the church in flashes and glimpses. It's there in moments. In, like, whippets of time."

"That is so sad."

"Is it? Look. I think if we can ask Christians to strive to be better, then why can't we ask homosexuals to strive to be better too. It's just sin like any other sin. We all fall short. Why should we say that we have to correct our sin, but them, they're just totally hunky-dory sinning their way as often as they want to do it, over and over. No. We have to repent. They have to repent. They're not different. They're not special."

"But it's not a sin."

"I just don't understand how you can possibly say that. You know the Bible as well as I do."

"Well . . . if the Holy Spirit is only in our churches in little bits and flashes, then what can we do to get it to sustain? How can we have more Holy Spirit?"

"Um . . . I think . . . we have to see the church as being more than just a building. The church is all around us. Like Tozer says, all of Creation is a sanctuary. Every moment, no matter where we are or what we're doing is an opportunity to worship."

"What does that mean?"

"It means whatever you do, whether you eat or drink, do it all to the glory of God."

"Well, I think we need to be more loving. More compassionate. We need to share Christ's love with everyone, whether we like them or not. Whether we agree with them or not. Whether we think they're sinners or not. We have to love them. That's how we get more Holy Spirit."

"Well . . . Amen." He nodded his head. "You preach it, Katie! We need more love. Less judgement. More love."

Just then, the tractor started up with a rumble. A rainbow flash puffed in the exhaust from the John Deere's muffler pipe and then disappeared like the Holy Spirit passing through hands at a Pentecostal worship service.

Katie wiped a tear from her cheek. Dave put his arm around her and drew her closer to him. Her body melted into him. And the tractor drove up the hillside into the sun.

When they arrived at the grove of Canaan Firs, it felt surprisingly warm. They stepped down off the wagon, and Dave took off his hat and gloves and shoved them into the pockets of his coat.

The tractor driver walked around to meet them behind the wagon.

"Hey. I'm Bill," he told them. He handed Dave a bow saw and a paper ticket. He explained that once they pick their tree, they can cut it down themselves. Then, they just pull the tree out to a place marked with a "Tractor Stop" sign. They tag the tree with one half of the ticket. They keep the other half. Then, when they head back to the entrance of the farm, they'll be reunited with their tree. Dave explained to him that they needed six trees. The driver pulled five more tickets out of his coat pocket.

"Thank you," David told him.

The driver hopped back up on the tractor and headed back down the hill, leaving Dave and Katie completely alone on the mountainside with nothing but snow, evergreen trees, and a bright, shimmering sky. The sun shocked their eyes, bounding off the whiteness of the snow.

Together, they stepped quietly through the maze of tree stumps left behind by a season of pickers. When they crested another layer of hillside, they could see for miles, and it was so quiet that Dave figured they could hear the wind rushing way down in the valley far below where the tiny car was parked by the tiny house. And there were evergreen trees as far as the eye could see.

Katie picked a noble-looking fir tree, and David cut it down. They dragged it over to the tractor stop. Then, they moved over to the Blue Spruce grove and cut down three of those. They liked the bluish tint and the softness of the needles. In the Scotch Pine grove, they found two more. When they were all done, they decided to just take their time and walk back down the mountain. They walked hand in hand. For a while, they both just watched the birds fly from tree to tree. As they walked, their strides slowly fell into rhythm with each other until the sound of their shoes crunching in the snow completely synced up. Suddenly, they both noticed a kind of music in the air around them.

Dave started singing, "Before I spoke a word, you were singing over me. You have been so so good to me."

At the chorus, Katie joined in with a vocal harmony that laid gently on top of his melody. "Oh the overwhelming, never ending, reckless love of God . . ."

And they sang their way down the mountain. The longer they sang, the louder their voices got. The final verse blasted out from their lungs and rose up into the heavens. And they danced along in the snowy groves of evergreen trees.

When they finally got back to the farm entrance, their six trees had already been shaken and bundled. Next, the farm workers tied them all down to their trailer. But before leaving, Dave and Katie decided to check out the little Christmas shop. It was a tiny storefront, but they had some really cool stuff. The couple sipped some hot chocolate and picked out three wreaths and a handful of handmade Christmas ornaments. The ornaments reminded them both of Katie's Mom's handmade ornaments.

When they got back in Dave's car, they weren't even down the lane yet to the main road when he turned to her and asked, "You wanna go see Rainmaker Cross?"

She smiled in a such a way that the sunlight turned and radiated over to him. He could feel the warmth of it. "Yes," she said without ever changing the shape of her smile.

Rainmaker Cross was at the top of Rainmaker Mountain, which was in the town of Stallings, PA, about a 45-minute drive east. Legend has it that back in the day, in the early 1900's, there was a severe draught in the area that devastated the land and burned up all the crops. There was a local farmer named John Stallings whose family had nearly starved to death. Their youngest daughter was extremely weak. In desperation, he built a thirty-foot cross out of the tallest red cedars he could find. The legend goes that he carried that cross up the side of Rainmaker Mountain to the very top, and he stuck it there in the ground for the whole world to see. All night, he prayed for rain at the foot of the cross, and by morning, the skies had opened, and the rains finally came.

A couple decades ago, the State came in and made the site into a historic landmark. They built a little park and made a hiking trail that supposedly follows old John Stallings path up the mountain.

Dave and Katie both relaxed and settled in for the car ride. They listened to Dave's playlist, and with the tension slowly melting away, they were able to enjoy and appreciate his musical choices. Rich Mullins, Jars of Clay, Shane and Shane. Each song reached into their hearts in some way.

For a long while, they sat quietly, staring out the car windows, watching the familiar landscape drift by. They were in the Appalachian foothills, and the landscape was very jagged and hilly. The white blanket of snow made it look different. Calm. Peaceful. But there was still something familiar about it. There were no other cars on these back roads and very few houses. Just trees and trees and trees. Occasionally, a thick-furred deer would look up from its foraging along the road and gracefully dart off into the woods with a pulse of muscles.

There was a barn that they both noticed up on a hillside. It was a white barn or at least it used to be. There was a time when it would have blended right into the snow. But over the many decades, the siding of the barn had been weathered by the elements. There was a pattern of grayness on the side of the barn that wasn't random but it also wasn't symmetrical. It strained your eyes if you looked at it wrong. The whiter parts of it melted into the snow. The darker parts popped out, almost like a 3D painting, so that it didn't even look like a barn at all but some kind of monstrous creature trying desperately to hide in plain sight.

Dave noticed the barn first, since it was on his side of the road. In his mind, the barn represented people. It was never pure white, never as white as the snow. It was always slightly off color. Slightly out of alignment, which made him think of the concept of original sin. We were always separated from God, because all of Creation is fallen. Even the whiteness of the snow isn't as pure as the holiness of Heaven. The older we get, the more stained our lives become from sin. Our only hope is Christ.

A few seconds later, Katie noticed the barn too. In her mind, we all start out pure white like that barn must have started out when it was first painted. We were all once perfect little babies, just as God created us. Over time, the winds of this world beat against us and change us into slightly off-white. Just a little gray in our hearts and minds. Slightly off from the way God had made us to be. In Katie's mind, the winds of the world made us cold and unloving and fearful. Those were the things that separated us from God. Those were our sins.

"Do you still listen to worship music and Christian music," Dave asked suddenly.

"Of course. I'm still me."

"I know. But, I mean. Has your taste in music changed at all? Are you listening to any other types of music that you weren't before?"

"Well . . ." She gazed out the window at the white, shivering trees. "I guess I listen to more hip hop now."

"Hip Hop? Really?"

"Yeah."

"Like who're you listening to?"

"Kendrick Lamar . . ."

"What? Why?"

"He's good. He really has something to say. He's a poet. He won like a Pulitzer Prize or something."

"Yeah, but . . . What is it that you think he has to say?"

"I don't know. I think he has insight into the African-American experience. And I think he tells it in a compelling way. He's a storyteller."

"Maybe." Dave was not convinced. He shifted in his seat and moved his hands lower on the steering wheel. "Does your new friend, Ariel, listen to Hip Hop?"

"Yes."

"Uh-huh."

"What?"

"I see now."

"What?"

"He's such a dude."

"What're you talking about?"

"Hip Hop is for dudes."

"That's not true at all."

"Kendrick Lamar." He shook his head. "Got famous from calling another rapper a pedophile."

"He was famous way before that."

"Ok." He adjusted the heater on the dashboard. It was too hot in the car. He turned the heat down and took off his hat—tossed it in the backseat.

They rode along in silence until they reached the town of Stallings. They passed the "Welcome to Stallings" sign. It wasn't any bigger than a folded-up newspaper. Dave turned onto Rainmaker Lane, the only road on the northern slope of Rainmaker Mountain. His car twisted up the winding gravel road. Pebbles pinged off the undercarriage and kicked out under the tires. Katie saw a dark, red fox dive down into a hole in the earth as Dave parked the car at the trailhead. There was a another, small, blue sign that simply said, "Trail Head."

They both got out of the car and thumped their doors shut. Together, they started up the gravely, snow-covered trail. The trail was very steep and narrow. The outdoor temperature was much warmer now. Dave took off his hat and gloves and shoved them in the pockets of his coat. Katie did the same. There was water dripping from the trees as the snow in the branches slowly melted. They could hear the beads of water tapping in the snow all around.

The trail was dark from the denseness of trees. Dark like the sun was setting even though it was only one in the afternoon. But the sunlight still sneaked through the branches above and slashed and slanted along the ground, striking unexpected shapes and patterns in the snow that shifted and twisted as the branches above swayed in the wind.

"So I was thinking about the story of Rainmaker Cross," Dave said. "And how it was a devastating drought. He built the cross, and carried it to the top of the mountain and he prayed all night long for rain. Then, in the morning, miraculously, it started raining. It saved his farm and his family . . ."

"Yeah."

"Do you still believe God can work miracles?"

"Um," she began. "I think it's a miracle all of this exists." She gestured to everything all around, the trees, the snow, the earth, the sky. Everything. "And I think it's a miracle every time a baby is born. I guess my answer is yes. I think that miracles happen all the time."

"Do you believe God answers prayers? That he makes miracles happen to answer prayers?"

"Well . . ." She looked down at her shoes in the snow. The snow was melting and turning to slush, so her footsteps sounded wet. "I don't know. I don't know what I think about prayer. I know that God cares about us. I think that God listens. I guess . . . well. I guess I would say that God works through circumstances to answer prayers. And people. God works through people to answer prayer. We are His hands and feet. It's through us loving and caring for people that their prayers are answered. I don't know. What do you think about prayer?"

"I guess I've been struggling with prayer a little bit too." He reached his hand up to his chin and noticed that he had some stubble starting to grow in. "But I do believe that words are powerful. There's a passage in the

Bible where it says that words are seeds. And then in Genesis 1, in the very beginning, God speaks, and His words bring about all of Creation. So His words are like the seeds of everything. Everything around us. But I think that our words are seeds too. They are important. Powerful. They have an impact on the world around us too. A smaller impact but still. And I think that's why prayer is important, because we have to put into words all of the most . . . the deepest things that are weighing the most on our hearts and minds. And if we keep praying, keep casting those seeds, then eventually. I don't know. I guess eventually something will grow."

"By that you mean that God will intervene in some miraculous way?"

"Yeah."

"But what about all those people out there who live and suffer and die and nothing ever changes. God never intervenes. They pray. Their families pray. And God is silent. The homeless guy living under a bridge. Or that woman in an abusive relationship she feels trapped in."

He shrugged. "I can't answer that. But have you ever said a prayer and like really felt, like deeply felt that God was listening? That He was there?"

"I guess so. Maybe."

"Maybe sometimes that's God's answer to prayer. Just to comfort us in our time of struggle. We have to go through it, but He's there going through it with us too."

"But why," she asked quickly. "If he truly loves us and if He can actually do anything, then why on earth would He not just snap His fingers or send a lightning bolt and help us? If He knows we're hurting, why wouldn't He take the pain away?"

"I don't know. Sometimes we just gotta go through it. Sometimes, it's the struggles and the pain that refine us, conform us into who God created us to be. Sometimes, I think, we just need to go through it."

"But don't you just think there's something so cold and uncaring about Creation? The whole predator and prey concept. And I remember in my dorm room at college when I was a freshman. We had bird's nest right there on our window ledge on the third floor. It was like the most beautiful thing I'd ever seen. The baby birds were so cute and, like, alien-looking. One day, they were all gone out of the nest, and we all thought they must've just flown away. But when I went to class, I saw two of those beautiful, little birds dead and split open on the sidewalk. I'll never forget it. It was horrifying! How do you reconcile that with a loving God?"

"Babe," he shrugged. "We live in a fallen world."

"Simple as that?"

"Simple as that."

"But God knew Adam and Even were gonna sin. He created them to sin. How can you just let Him off the hook for that? How can you just say that it's all settled and fine. That's so small, David. It makes you seem uncaring and unsympathetic to all the pain and suffering in the world."

"But Katie. Look at all the beauty around you. God's Creation is beautiful. And He created us. We're here to enjoy it, to drink it in, to take care of it, to keep it beautiful. That's a miracle. It might be hard and sad and tragic. But it's also beautiful and amazing and miraculous. And the beauty is more beautiful because of the sadness. The miracles are more miraculous because of the tragedies. This is just life."

"I don't necessarily disagree with that," she said. "Something I was thinking about. I do think that God can and does work through miracles. But I think that mostly, He works through natural processes. Through other people. Through circumstances. Like, I feel like the earth is billions of years old. That we did evolve. That evolution and natural selection is the path God used to get us all here."

"So you think the first chapter of Genesis is just a metaphor?"

"Yes. It's a story. Was never meant to be taken literally."

"I don't know."

"I've even heard my Dad say from the pulpit if you don't believe in a literal six-day Creation then you don't have the right or the correct understanding of the Gospel. And I just think that's trash. Just because someone doesn't agree with you doesn't mean that they're not saved or not Christian or that they don't understand the Gospel."

"But there is objective Truth in the world. And He gives it to us in His Word."

"But, David, we're all different. We're gonna read it differently. And that needs to be ok, because it's true. We all have different interpretations of every single passage in the Bible, because we all have different perspectives, different life experiences, different DNA."

"Ok, but let me ask you this. What do you think the Bible is?"

"I think it's a library of books written by Jewish men who were . . . earnestly . . . trying to understand life and make sense of God."

"Ok. But do you think it's the Word of God?"

"I mean. Yes."

"You think the Jewish men who wrote were inspired by God?"

"Well, I mean. What do you mean by that?"

"I mean they were the instruments of God in order to deliver His Word to us today and to all future generations so that we know how we need to live, what we need to believe so we can be saved."

"David, honestly, it seems to me like you're just using a bunch of religious language that isn't really all that helpful. Just jargon that confuses people and makes people feel uncomfortable."

"What religious language are you talking about?"

"Word of God. Inspired by God. Saved. These're all just words."

"They're not just words. They're seeds. Seeds that God plants in our lives to help us learn and grow and expand our hearts and our minds."

"Or they could be more like bricks we use to build a wall of beliefs and doctrine that we stack up and hide behind and use to keep away all the wrong things and the wrong people."

"That's a pretty interesting analogy," he said.

"It's a Rob Bell analogy. I think it was from his first book. He talks about Christians building walls brick by brick out of what they think are the right beliefs. But that wall keeps people out. He said Christianity should be more like a trampoline. And we're all just jumping and living free and loving life. And everyone else sees us all having fun and enjoying life, and they wanna join us, because it looks amazing."

"But don't you think it's both. It's like a little bit of both. You need both to live out the Christian faith."

"I guess I hadn't thought of it that way."

"Yeah."

"But don't you think there's too much focus, like, among Christians. Too much focus on believing the right things? I don't think that's what Jesus was about. He was about transformation and living a different life. Letting a relationship with God change your heart on the inside so that the way you go through life changes. You treat people differently. You love with a deeper sense from a deeper place in your heart."

"I don't disagree with that. Be doers of the Word and not just hearers."

"That's exactly right. We get so caught up in believing the right things that we forget to do the right things in the world, the right things for the people around us. We forget to live it out."

"I see what you mean."

"I heard this story on a podcast recently. There's this guy and he's on trial for being a Christian. And the prosecutor is presenting all this evidence against him. . ."

"Ok."

"And the guy's all nervous, because he thinks the evidence is airtight. All the Bibles that were found at his house. All the hymnals and devotional books and tracts. His church membership certificate. All these things. And it's time for the judge to make his ruling, and the guy's sweating. He's nervous, because he knows the judge is gonna find him guilty. Finally, the judge looks him in the eyes and says, I find you innocent. And the guy's completed stunned. Shocked. And he says, what? Why? And the judge tells him, look man. I didn't see any evidence of you helping the poor or the needy. I didn't see any evidence of you loving your neighbor. I didn't see any evidence of you living out the Great Commission or being the Good Samaritan. No evidence of you living out the lessons of Christ."

"Yeah. I mean I see that we can sometimes get caught up in looking like we're a good Christian rather than actually being more Christlike."

"Yeah. Totally."

"But Baby, that's just 'cuz people suck. We can live out this Christian walk the way we want to, the way we believe is right. It's between us and God. Not between us and any of them."

"Yeah. You're right. But do you think that the church is the right place to do that? Do you think we need the church?"

"I do. Absolutely."

"But it's just so easy to get caught up in comparing yourself to others and trying to out-Christian the Christian next to you."

"Then we pray about it. We ask God to keep us on track. Keep us focused on Him and not the people around us. No church is perfect. There is no true church."

"But don't you think the church is doing more harm than good?"

"No way! The Christian Church is the largest healthcare provider in the world, outside of government."

"Well, I didn't know that."

"Yeah. And I mean. There is no Big-C, Christian church. It's just a bunch of very loosely-connected local churches. If you don't like one, you just try a different one."

"But what if they all suck?"

"Well no one is ever gonna find a church that they completely agree with. I think if you do, then maybe you need to think a little deeper. Make God a little more personal. You just need to find a church that both challenges and encourages you."

"Do you really think so?"

"Yes."

"I don't know." Katie looked up into the bright, blue sky as a woodpecker flicked from branch from branch. "Well. Hey. What do you think the Bible actually is?"

"Uh . . . that's heavy question." He looked down at his boots in the snow. "I guess I'll go back to words as seeds. The Bible is the Word of God. It's seeds that God plants in our soul in the hopes that they one day blossom into something beautiful and amazing in our lives."

She looked over at him and smiled. "You and your seeds," she said as she slapped her hand against his chest. Not hard but harder than he expected.

"The Bible Project calls the Bible a unified story that leads to Jesus, and I think. . ."

"No way! I love the Bible Project," she told him. "It's a beautiful idea. A unified story."

"Yeah. I agree."

"Have you ever heard of Dan McClellan," Katie asked.

"Who?"

"Dan McClellan."

"No."

"Now, I agree with the Bible Project about a unified story, but Dan has a different take on the Bible, and I don't disagree with him either. He talks about the univocality of the Bible."

"I've heard of that word. It's about, like, the Bible, like, speaks in one voice. A consistent and unified voice."

"Yeah. Exactly. He says that there is no univocality to the Bible. He says that there are hundreds of inconsistencies and contradictions in the Bible and that each writer has a different perspective and different ideas and that all these diverse voices can't all, like, meld together into one voice."

"He sounds like a fun guy."

"Yeah," she laughed. "He's a pretty serious dude."

"But I think the point of the Bible Project is that in spite of all that diversity and differences and passage of time, God works it all together to tell the story, to unfold the story. The one story. I heard Tim Mackie, from the Bible Project, one time explain it like the Bible is an orchard. Over here there's apple trees and cherry trees, and over there, there's strawberry bushes and grape vines. On the surface, it looks very different and diverse. But underground, all those roots are connected and like braided together. When you dig deep enough, you see it's all actually one."

"That's beautiful! Isn't Tim the best?"

"Yeah. Totally."

They were walking through the tunnel of birch trees, so they knew they were near the end of the trail.

"Race ya to the cross," Katie said. And she took off running. Her shoes squished in the wet snow. The wind rushed against her face and wrestled her hair in every direction. She felt free and fast. She heard Dave running behind her. He was close behind.

They ran for much longer than they expected, and they were both breathing heavy. They had misjudged how long the tunnel of birch trees was. It was really long. Suddenly, Katie stopped and Dave stopped beside her, and they bent over, catching their breath together, side by side. Katie was hot, sweating. She unzipped her coat and tied it around her waist. She ran her fingers through her hair. And then, she took off running again.

Finally, they made it to the cross. They threw themselves down into the melting snow, and they lay there on their backs so close their hair was touching. And they looked up into the sky together, laughing.

Eventually, Katie jumped to her feet and Dave came with her. They stood at the edge of the clearing, about 25 feet ahead of the cross, at the top of Rainmaker Mountain, and they gazed down at the view. It was spectacular. They could see for miles and miles. Into three other counties from that one spot.

"This is it," Katie said. "This is the wonder of God's Creation. This is all the miracle we need. We don't need to believe in the Trinity or original sin or eternal salvation or the coming tribulation. Those beliefs are all idols. They're idols. They're distractions from this. The Word of God right here in our midst."

Dave didn't say anything. He was looking at her. He wasn't looking out at the view. When she turned to look at him, their eyes locked. She held his gaze for a long time. Long enough for the sun to start its setting. Finally, he kissed her. It started out as a hard, passionate kiss. Their bodies were bending and swaying like trees blowing together in the wind. It was quick and tense and out of sync. Slowly, it melted into a soft, loving kiss nested inside of a warm, gentle embrace. Their bodies slipped slowly into place like puzzle pieces, and they become part of the landscape there on the mountain. Roots grew from their feet and anchored in the earth. Branches emerged from their hair and reached into the sky and followed the red trail of the sun. Birds nested in their branches, and they were happy there together as one.

Before it got too dark, they decided to walk back down the trail. They were quieter going down. Katie was dying of thirst, as if Dave had kissed all the wetness from her mouth. It was getting a little colder as the sun slowly went down. She put her coat back on and zipped it up.

They were about halfway down the mountain when Dave stopped and turned to her. At first, she thought he was going to kiss her again, but he didn't.

"But you do believe that Jesus is the son of God, right, and that he saved us from our sins," he asked her out of the blue, with the intensity of the sunset burning in his eyes.

She swallowed dryly. "Dave," she started. "I'm trying to leave all that evangelical language behind me. It's not helpful for me anymore. It's holding me back. It's actually hurting people that I care about who carry a lot of trauma from their upbringing in the church. That language is triggering for them."

"Are you talking about Ariel?"

"Yes."

"Katie, it's not just language to me. It's not holding me back. It's not triggering for me."

"I know."

"They're not just words. They're seeds," he told her. "I really believe that. Seeds that God planted deep in my heart when I read the Bible when I was a little boy and when I went to church when I was young. And those seeds are blooming in my heart and growing, Katie, and they're starting to turn into something beautiful in my life. And some of the branches are gonna die and rot. But some of them are gonna grow strong and bear fruit. I believe it, Katie."

"I know you do."

"Why don't you believe that for you? Why aren't the seeds growing for you?"

"I don't know." She looked away. "But I think I'm growing. I'm bloom-ing too. It's just not quite the same as you. It was different seeds I guess that took hold in my heart."

He reached for her hand, and their fingers slipped together like two streams of water.

"I'm scared," he told her. It was almost a whisper.

"Me too."

"I don't understand what's happening."

"I don't either." She stood up on her tiptoes and kissed him. It was a soft, gentle kiss, but it took a lot of their strength. And they were both worn out. Hand in hand, they walked back to Dave's car.

∾

They were both dying of thirst, but there wasn't a convenience store or anything in Stallings. They managed to find a restaurant. They saw a big wooden sign nailed to two trees with "T.T.'s Smokehouse" carved into the wood. Dave turned down a gravel drive. It was dark. There was a brick smokehouse with smoke tumbling out of a tall chimney. Next to it, was a pavilion with a corrugated metal roof where there must be outdoor seating in the summer. Connected to the pavilion was a small, shaker-sided build-ing not much bigger than the smokehouse.

They walked into the restaurant hand in hand. They drank water from mason jars and asked for refills before they even ordered. They were both so tired. There were no other customers. They each ordered the brisket and mac and cheese.

"Do you really think Christian beliefs are idols," he asked her softly.

"I think they can be. If they distract you from the calling of being the hands and feet of Christ. If they hold you back from becoming the person that God had created you to be."

He leaned forward over the table toward her. "But how is that pos-sible? Our beliefs are specifically intended to help Christians live out pre-cisely those two things. Beliefs are central to what faith is. They're central to walking a Christlike walk."

"I think that's how it was originally intended, but I think we've turned the beliefs into idols. We care more about what we believe than how we treat people. We care more about who believes the same things we do than how we can help others. These central Christian beliefs are turning us in-ward instead of turning us outward to love God and love our neighbor."

"Baby, I just don't see it. I mean I guess I see how it could happen. And maybe it does happen to some people. There are even a few guys from seminary who I can kind of see their reflection in everything that you're saying, but that doesn't mean that we would be any better off abandoning these beliefs. We just have to find better ways of living them out. Better ways for us."

"Maybe that's true," she shrugged.

"And how else will we know we're going in the right direction? That we're heading toward God and not just following the world, living the way the world lives?"

"By living out the words of Christ. To love God and love our neighbor. To lay down our lives for our friends. To take up our cross daily and follow Him. These are active callings. We have to be doers and not just hearers. I think that's something that James meant. Hearers quibble over doctrine and theology. They argue over interpretations. Doers don't do any of that, because they're living it out. They're doing it. They're being His hands and feet."

"I think it also has to be about a relationship. Because there's a billion different ways to do what you're describing. And how do you know which way is right for you. Which way is God calling you toward? Where does He need you?"

"I guess so. I don't really disagree. But I think we as Christians can just get too caught up in finding God's will for our lives. And we agonize over where we should go to school and what we should study and who we should marry. Like if we make one single mistake along the way, then we somehow aren't within His will for our lives."

"Yeah?"

"But maybe His will isn't that prescribed. It's just that He wants us to love Him and love others. All those other details are just distractions from that. They're just idols."

"I don't think so. I think those details are exactly how we live out the commandments to love God and love others. To love God, you have to live that out in the details. You have to be obedient to Him. You have to follow the plans He has for you. He has to be in the center of all your decisions. He has to be there in everything you do."

She looked down at her cloth napkin and wound it tightly around her fingers.

"Like this menu," he continued, lifting the laminated menu from the center of the table. "It's not a menu unless you have ribs on here and brisket on here and mac and cheese. Those details are the menu. If it was just a blank piece of paper that just said "menu" or whatever, then it's just not a menu."

"I don't know if I fully understand what you're saying. But it sounds to me like way too much pressure for us to put on ourselves. Way too much pressure for God to put on us. It's too much."

"Sure," he shrugged. "We're gonna fall short. That's why we need a Savior. But it's something we can strive for. We can't just throw all the details of life out the window and say, God is love. Peace, love, and donuts. I'm fine. You're fine. Everybody's fine."

"But don't you think that God loves us just as we are?"

"Yes. Of course. He died for us. But the Christian life is about seeking and striving and working and praying to be more like Christ in everything we do, no matter how small."

The waitress, who looked like she was about 14 years old, came over with their food. She dropped their plates down in front of them, and they ate. They took four bites before taking a breath.

"This is so good," Dave mumbled as he chewed the brisket.

Katie nodded in response. They both ate without talking until their plates were empty.

After dinner, they went out into the darkness. The restaurant had very little exterior lighting. They walked slowly arm in arm, like a blind couple, until they bumped into Dave's Mazda. Once he got in the car and started up the engine, the dashboard lights popped on, and everything was fine. Their anxiety dissipated.

The headlights pierced out into the dark and seemed to cut the night as they traveled. The roads were dark and windy, so Dave drove slow.

When they got to the town of Howling Run, there were some lights— houses and businesses lit up. Howling Run was a small town in the foothills that was known for its arts school, which taught primitive crafts like blacksmithing, glass blowing, and pottery as well as fine arts like painting, poetry, and sculpture. The school was tucked away back in the woods on the banks of Howling Run Creek. Across the creek from the school was an ancient Native American burial ground, and the students were known to swim across the creek and dig for artifacts for inspiration. The school itself resembled a backwater, colonial village with small houses used as classrooms, and a large churchlike building in the center, which acted like a gallery of sorts to display the students' best artwork.

Driving past the art center made Katie think of her best friend, Chloe. Chloe had worked at the school for years as an instructor. She even lived there for a short time after her mom died. Her shoulders sagged, thinking on how much she missed Chloe.

∾

Twenty minutes later, they pulled into Katie's driveway. They were both exhausted.

Dave walked Katie to her door. Side by side, they climbed the steps onto the porch. The porch light flicked on as they approached the door. He held her hand and kissed her. The porch light flickered.

"See you tomorrow," Katie told him.

"Love you."

"Love you too."

Katie creaked open the screen door and pulled out her keys. She turned the lock and entered the house. It was quiet. Her parents were asleep, so she kicked off her shoes without a sound.

Worn out by her long and harrowing conversation with Dave, which is still far from over, she trudged up the stairs to her bedroom, and threw on some cozy pajamas. She had intended to replay parts of the conversation in her head and analyze it, but instead, she fell fast asleep.

Dave's mind was buzzing with all the words that he and Katie had passed back and forth over the course of the day. It was overwhelming. His shoulders fell. He breathed out slowly. Out of the corner of his eye, he saw a flash of light against Katie's house.

Then, his foot slipped on a patch of ice, and he was suddenly looking up at the stars. They were falling all around him and moving fast like snowflakes in a storm. He didn't feel his head hit the sidewalk. He heard it. Like an egg cracking on the side of a cast iron skillet. One of the falling stars crashed into him with a startling burst of light, which fizzled to a deep, haunting black, and all the air in his body forsook his lungs in a single, violent, dark breath. He was stretched out on the sidewalk just a few steps from the gravel driveway, where the grainy halo of the porchlight began to fade.

∾

Katie startled awake with a quick, sharp intake of breath. Was there a sound? What was that? She was clutching her chest, her heart fluttering. Her hair shook when she sat up. She felt it brush her cheeks. There was a heavy silence. The air in the room was thick. She licked it from her lips. She felt a pressure in her chest. She walked down the stairs and ducked through the doorway at the bottom.

First, she went to the window in the living room, where she noticed that Dave's Mazda was still parked under the willow tree. She started biting her thumbnail. She ripped her thumb away and clamped it in her pocket. Then, she ran up the stairs to her room and grabbed her cell phone off the charger. She called him, but there was no answer. Her teeth were grinding.

Next, she went to the window in the kitchen. It was mostly dark. The porchlight had kicked off. Quickly, she grabbed her coat and pulled on her mom's muck boots. She went out onto the porch. The screen door screeched and then slapped shut. The wind was blowing. The only other sound she could hear was the gutters rattling.

Behind the house was a hayfield, but there was nothing growing there now. It was just a vast slant of dark blues cascading together in the wind. There was a crescent moon of light in the black sky that looked like it was hung a nail.

She pulled out her phone and called him again. She started biting her thumbnail.

She heard a cell phone ring. And the wind stopped whispering in her ear. She turned her head. It rang again. Her eyes moved toward the sound. Her feet shuffled. It rang again. That's when she saw a pin of light open up in the dark and then slowly disappear. She ran to the sound. She found him. Unconscious. There was blood. He was still breathing.

She picked up her phone to call 9-1-1, but then she remembered when she was a girl, Miley, the neighbor girl who lived on the horse ranch. She got kicked by a horse and broke her ribs. It took the ambulance over an hour. They got lost on the back roads on the way to Picture Creek. There were never any signposts on most of the roads. She would drive him to the hospital herself—could get there in half an hour.

She tried to lift him but couldn't. Just dead weight. She ran to the house and pulled her dad's car keys from the candy dish in the kitchen. She ran to her parents' bedroom and flung open the door. She shook her dad awake.

"Dad. I need you," she whispered.

"Huh?"

"I need your help. Get up."

He creaked to his feet and stepped into his slippers. He grabbed his robe from the wall hook and pulled it on. As he fumbled with his glasses, he found the words to ask, "What's wrong, Kitty?"

"Dave fell. Let's go!"

Groggy, he shuffled out into the living room. Katie grabbed him by the hand and pulled him along faster than his feet would go. He stumbled, but it jolted him awake.

They went outside and found him right where Katie had left him. Her dad lifted him by the shoulder, and Katie lifted his legs. They carried him over to the Jetta and shoved him into the backseat

"You takin' him to St.Ben's?"

She nodded.

"I'll go with you."

"No," she told him. "Stay here with mom. I need you to call his parents and have them meet us there."

"Ok."

"Then get dressed. Get mom up and meet us there too."

"You can count on me, Firefly."

"Thanks, dad." She hugged him and jumped into the driver's seat. She could hear her dad speaking a prayer as she closed the car door.

She hadn't driven in a while. She peeled out and kicked up some dirt and rocks. After that, she settled in and steered the Jetta down the steep driveway and out onto Hemlock Lane.

She drove, her knuckles burning around the wheel, faster than was probably safe in the dark on the windy roads, but she knew there would be no other traffic at this time of night. Tires squealed around turns and kicked up gravel, but she was focused. Her eyes were hard and bright inside the darkness of the car.

She got to St. Benedict's Hospital in 22 minutes. She pulled up to the front door and screamed for help, banging on the hood until a security guard came out to help. Within two minutes, a paramedics team had Dave in a wheelchair and were wheeling him into the Emergency Room. Katie ran behind them, answering their questions as they rushed down a hallway. An ER doctor ran over and asked her rapid fire questions. The doctor's face was eerily close to hers. Katie could smell her coffee breath. Katie hated the smell of coffee.

The paramedics turned a corner, and a nurse grabbed Katie by the arm.

"You need to stay here for right now," the nurse told her. "You can't go back there."

That's when Katie started to cry. It came out in spurts. The first tear landed on her wrist, and she felt it slide down her index finger. She collapsed into a chair in the waiting room and passed out.

When she came to, she was sitting about as awkwardly as anyone has ever sat. Her hips were twisted and pressed against one arm of the chair. Her back and neck were bent, and her face was pressed against the other arm of the chair.

In that moment, God brought the words of a Psalm into her heart. Psalm 32:7: "You are my hiding place. You will protect me from trouble and surround me with songs of deliverance."

She hummed a little tune and then fell asleep.

She woke up in the hospital waiting room. It was close to midnight. A pot of coffee was brewing somewhere. Katie stretched out her arms and legs but didn't bother getting up out of the chair. She looked around the waiting room. It was mostly empty. There were five people. They were all looking down at their cell phones, so she couldn't really see their faces. Her eyes settled on a little girl, about five, dressed in a furry pink coat. She was playing a game on her phone. She had cute, blonde pigtails. Katie wondered for a moment if this image of the little girl in the furry, pink coat would be something she would remember ten years from now.

The carpet was dark blue, and it had a pattern of diamonds on it. There was a dark stain near her foot where someone had spilled pop or fruit juice or something a long time ago. She could hear the hum of vending machines before she even saw them. They were over beside the reception desk.

"Katie!"

It was her dad. She leapt up out of the chair, spun around to see him, and fell into his arms. Immediately, she was crying on his shoulders.

"Sweetie," he said. "My Katie. It's gonna be ok. He's gonna be alright. It's all gonna be alright. The Lord is watching over us. He will never leave us nor forsake us. He is our shepherd. We having nothing to fear. He is with us."

When Katie opened her eyes, she noticed her mom standing there. She was smiling, but her eyes were sad.

"Hi mom."

"Hi, sweetie." Her mom reached out and placed her hand gently on Katie's shoulder.

Finally, Katie pulled out of her father's hug. He would've held her in that hug forever if she'd wanted him to. He would've skipped meals. He would've stood there even if the arthritis in his knee burned and ached to high heaven. But she pulled away, and he tried his best to smile.

Katie saw the doctor across the room. She took off running and caught up to her in an adjacent hallway. The doctor wasn't turning around even though she had to have heard Katie's footsteps coming up on her fast. Katie reached out to touch her on the shoulder. It was all happening fast, but just before her hand touched the doctor's shoulders, time slowed down, and Katie had a thought that maybe she was in a movie. Or maybe it was a dream, and none of this was actually happening. Maybe the doctor wasn't really there. Maybe she would ripple and vanish before her hand could touch her. And Katie would wake up in her bed. And everything would be just fine.

Katie's hand touched the cotton fabric of the white coat the doctor was wearing over her scrubs. The doctor's body tensed for a moment, and Katie could feel it. Then, the woman turned to face her quickly.

"Oooh," the doctor said. "You scared me." She was short, early thirties, with thick, red hair pulled back into a long ponytail. "Are you the one who came in with David Ecchols?"

"Yes. Is he ok?"

"Well, he's conscious and alert. You should be able to see him in a few minutes. But he definitely has a concussion, and he may have suffered more extensive damage. He was unconscious and unresponsive for so long. So I ordered him a CT scan, and they should be coming to get him for that test within the hour. If you could just go back and sit in the waiting room for another minute, I'll make sure the nurses know that he's ready for visitors."

And then she turned and went about her day.

～

Dave was uncomfortable. The hospital smelled funny. He couldn't put his finger on it. And the lights were so bright, he couldn't keep his eyes open more than a few seconds at a time. He had a pounding headache like he had never experienced before. He could feel like a tightness in his throat and a tingle down his arms. His mouth was intensely dry, but he had drunk through six cups of water, and it didn't help at all. So now he had to pee really bad, but he had zero interest in getting up to go to the bathroom.

He wasn't in a room. He was still in the ER. He had curtains pulled shut all around him, so he couldn't see anything outside of his space, but he could hear it all. The monitor by his bed kept beeping every few seconds, and whenever it did, he could feel it like a knife blade slashing the back of his brain.

He tried to lick his lips, but his tongue felt like sandpaper.

He couldn't remember what happened or how he ended up in the hospital. But he knew that he had been unconscious for some time, and he remembered having a dream while he was out. But all he could really remember of it were feelings and vague images. He remembered a hand. Katie's hand. He remembered the sound of a baby crying. He remembered a crescent moon of light in the middle of a dark floor. He remembered the smell of lasagna cooking. That was all he could remember.

He heard the curtain pulling back and assumed it was a nurse coming to check up on him. He ventured to slit open his eyes for a moment and saw Katie standing in front of him. His body tensed.

"No," he shouted. "Katie no." His voice sounded deformed and twisted like a tree that had been struck by lightning years ago. He couldn't think of any other words to say, and he didn't quite even know why he was saying the words that he was saying. "No," he shouted again. He covered his face with his hands. "No."

"What? Why? Why are saying that? Are you ok?" She reached for him, and he pulled away.

"Get out," he yelled. "Get out!"

~

Katie turned her back on him. She was crying. Before she left, she twisted her head to look back at him. He looked scared and tired and angry. His eyes were closed. She pulled the curtain shut and went back to the waiting room. Dave's parents were there. Before they could see her, she sneaked off down the hallway to the bathroom. Her shoes squeaked down the hall. The bathroom door creaked as she pulled it shut. She looked in the mirror and cried so she didn't have to feel alone.

~

Dave was feeling better. So good, in fact, he decided to get up and use the bathroom. When he sat up, he thought his head would feel like it was floating away on a balloon. But it didn't. It stayed attached. He swung his legs over the side of the bed and sat there a minute feeling the cold of the floor on his bare feet. Finally, he stood up and worked his way across over to the curtain. He was connected to a machine, which he had to wheel around in front of him.

When he pulled back the curtain, he was confused. It didn't look at all like he had imagined it in his mind. He found a nurse and asked her where the restroom was. On his way back from the restroom, he suddenly started thinking about the Apostle Paul and his vision on the Road to Damascus. He wondered about the vision. What might Paul have seen exactly that changed his life so dramatically? And Dave thought about the dream he had while he was knocked out. He really couldn't remember much of it, but he had this feeling like it was important. Like God was telling him something. He thought about how confrontational he had been with Katie just a little bit ago. He had never treated her like that in his entire life. But somehow it made him feel better, like it was something he needed to do.

When he came back from the restroom, he settled back onto the gurney and looked up at the lights. He really did feel so much better. He closed his eyes and a vision from his dream returned to him behind his eyes. He was working at his dad's engineering firm. Sitting at a computer. Taking a phone call. Entering data into a spreadsheet. There was a framed photograph on his desk of a mother with two little children, but the mother's face was torn out, and there was just a ragged white plastic backdrop where her face should be. The phone was ringing and ringing and ringing. And no one would answer it. Eventually, he realized that it was his phone. But he didn't want to answer.

He opened his eyes and pulled the sheets up to his chin.

With a loud, sudden whoosh, the curtain pulled, and a tall, muscular, intimidating nurse with a ponytail and tattoos down her arms said his name coldly.

"Yes?"

Without a word, she wheeled him off down the hallway for his CT Scan.

∼

Katie was in the waiting room biting her nails and grinding her teeth, while her parents and Dave's parents chatted and smiled politely with each other. It was like they were acting out vignettes from some sort of stage play. She couldn't hear anything they were saying, and honestly, she didn't want to know. There was a clock ticking somewhere. She could feel the sound of it in her teeth. Something was seriously wrong with Dave. Couldn't they see it? After her dad prayed with Dave's parents when they first arrived, they haven't said a single word about Dave. They're just blabbing on and on about the wedding. Wake up, people! He might have a traumatic brain injury! There might not be a wedding!

～

Dave was wheeled into a big, bright room. He laid down on a narrow, metal table. The table began to move, and he slid back into a tunnel. And he was looking up at the insides of a big machine. He thought of Jonah in the belly of the great fish.

The CT Technician spoke to him through an intercom system, but it came through all garbled, so he just responded, "Ok." Then, he closed his eyes and fell asleep. Or maybe he wasn't asleep, but he started dreaming. He dreamed of Katie. She looked a little older. A few gray hairs. A rounder face. She looked sad and tired. He reached out his hand to comfort her, but she slapped it away. "Don't touch me!" Then, suddenly, he was in a car. He was in a sport coat and tie. He was going to church. The passenger seat was empty, except for his acoustic case, which was sitting on the floor of the car and leaned back against the seat. He glanced up in the rear-view mirror and saw two little boys in their car seats. One was seven. The other was about four. They were both crying. "I miss, Mommy."

He woke up, and the intimidating nurse wheeled him back to the ER. He didn't even know her name. He tried to look at the name on her badge, but it was swinging and bouncing as she moved. He looked away, because he didn't want her think he was staring at her boobs. She could probably take him in a fight if it came to that.

～

Katie stood up quick, like a soldier, when the doctor came into the waiting room. She walked quickly up to Katie.

"The CT Scan looked great," she said, seeming almost chipper, with a flip of her hair.

Katie blinked.

"Honestly. I was shocked. There doesn't appear to be any damage at all," the doctor continued. "There's no internal bruising or bleeding. No fractures. I had multiple colleagues look it over to make I wasn't missing anything. The Scan is perfectly clear. Now . . . he does have a pretty serious concussion. So he's gonna experience headaches, nausea, dizziness, lack of energy, loss of appetite, things like that for a while. But his balance and coordination are good. His eye movement's good. Reflexes are normal. He's reading normally, speaking normally. His short-term memory is fine. He's doing remarkably well given how long he was unconscious."

Katie realized she was nodding her head. She had no idea for how long.

"It's incredibly important," the doctor added, "that he not sustain another head injury before this one is fully healed. I cannot stress to you enough how crucial this is. He should rest for at least the next week or so. He should move as little as possible over the next couple of days. He needs to avoid screens: phones, tv's, computer monitors. He shouldn't drive for at least a few days. He needs . . . to . . . rest."

"But we're getting married on Saturday," Katie said, her bottom lip quivering, her eyes welling over and shining in the fluorescent light.

"Oh, sweetie," said the doctor. "Congratulations! That's amazing! You marry that man. Just don't bonk him on the head. Ok?" She smiled.

And Katie smiled too, but she was still on the verge of tears.

"Look," the doctor continued. "Give us about ten minutes, and then he'll be ready to go home. He should follow-up with his PCP in about three days."

～

Dave walked out of St. Benedict's Hospital, very slowly. He raised his arm to shield his eyes from the glare of the lampposts. He refused to look at Katie. But he wasn't making eye contact with anyone, so she tried not to take it personally.

Slowly, he eased his body into the passenger seat of his Mazda. Katie's dad had driven it to the hospital. The Christmas trees were still on the trailer behind the vehicle. Dave's dad fell into the driver's seat beside him. He slapped his giant hand down on Dave's leg and grabbed him roughly just above the knee.

"Hey, kiddo," he said. "You gave your mom and I quite a scare. Your mom almost had a heart attack when Pastor Vreeland called us."

Dave didn't say anything. He honestly couldn't think of anything to say.

~

Katie was exhausted, but she tossed and turned for hours. She desperately wanted to take back everything she had said to Dave over the past few days. None of it mattered at all. She just wanted him. She wanted to make him happy. She wanted to be his wife. She wanted to love him and to be loved. She wanted to live for him. She wanted to have his children and raise them up with him. She wanted him to be the spiritual leader in their family. She wanted to follow him. These were the things she wanted more than anything. Honestly.

But she couldn't take it back. And, of course, she wanted to be honest with him. That's the kind of relationship she wanted, where they could both be completely honest with each other.

She kicked off the blankets and clenched her fists. She got up and paced the floor. Her teeth were grinding. She grabbed her phone. She typed out a text to Dave, "I love you!" She hit send. She threw the phone done on her bed.

~

Dave heard his phone buzz, but he wasn't supposed to look at screens, so he didn't even turn his head toward the sound. In fact, he didn't move at all. He just laid in bed like a sack of potatoes.

He couldn't really remember the dream he had when he was unconscious, just image shrapnel and flashes of feelings, but he felt them all in some elemental part of his body or his mind or spirit or something that he couldn't identify but he could feel. He believed the dream to be a vision from God, showing him what his life would be like if he marries Katie. It would be relentlessly hard and miserable and sad. Her newfound beliefs, or lack of beliefs, would prevent him from keeping a job in ministry anywhere, and he would end up working at his dad's firm. He would make good money and have a beautiful house and an expensive car, but it would slowly suffocate him every day. And then, he would come home to a family torn apart by their dysfunction. Filled with inconsistency and confusion. Their two, beautiful kids riddled with anxiety and uncertainty. They would grow up weak and afraid and angry at themselves without knowing why.

God had gifted him with a prophetic vision, and it was stark and dreadful. It wasn't exactly apocalyptic with trumpets and dragons and horsemen, but it was symbolic of the end times of something.

He remembered a stairwell in his dream. A stairwell in his future home with Katie. He was standing at the bottom and walking up, but the stairs ahead of him were twisting and bending so that he couldn't tell if he was going up or down.

Chapter 4

Tuesday

KATIE WOKE UP AT 10:30 in the morning. It seemed like a winter morning. She shivered when she pulled herself out from under the blankets. Her mind was buzzing and fizzing. She was getting married on Saturday. She would focus on that. There was so much to do between now and then, and Dave wouldn't be able to help her. She had planned for them to do it all together. Now, she was alone in it, and it was overwhelming for one person.

She was pacing the floor in her bedroom. Her teeth were grinding. She threw on a hoodie to stay warm. She grabbed her phone. Only one person could help now. She needed Chloe. Chloe had never failed her.

She sent Chloe a text, "Are you in town? I need you."

Immediately, a text came back, "Be there in 10."

In nine minutes and thirty-eight seconds, Chloe's shiny, new Jeep pulled in the driveway. She was staying in Howling Run, which was at least twenty minutes away, but she had made the drive in less than ten.

Chloe had been Katie's best friend since they were both in fourth grade. They went to school together until tenth grade when Chloe went away to boarding school in West Virginia. Her dad was a Neurosurgeon who had been the head of surgery at St. Benedict Hospital when they were kids, but then when Chloe's mom died, he poured himself into his job. He took a prestigious position at UPMC in Pittsburgh. Chloe refused to move with him, and she ended up living by herself for a while when she was only fourteen. She actually lived with Katie's family for a few months. Eventually, the family who owns Howling Run Center for the Arts took her in. She had been taking acting classes there since she was little. They let her live in one of the small buildings on the Howling Run campus. They checked in on her every day. She ate dinner at their house most nights. They gave her a part-time job teaching poetry and acting classes and cleaning up the buildings every night. Even now, every year, the Arts Center hosted an Open House, and Chloe would come back and shout her poetry from the rooftops while crowds of people toured the campus.

One other thing to know about Chloe is that she's a successful, Hollywood actor. She's not famous yet, but she has landed roles in big-budget, Hollywood movies. Recently, she scored her highest-profile gig yet as the lead in a highly-anticipated, new Netflix series. She has wrapped up filming, but the show won't be released for some time. Her phone, though, had been ringing off the hook with new opportunities.

Chloe jumped out of her fire-red Jeep and slammed the door. Katie came out to meet her in the driveway. When they made eye contact, there was a harmonized shriek that parted the clouds and shone the sun for a moment. They sprinted at each other and embraced. Chloe lifted Katie off her feet and kissed her on the cheek. They had not seen each other in person for over a year.

"What's up, baby? You look breathtaking gorgeous, my darling," Chloe shouted in a faux-British accent.

"And you are like big-time, Hollywood legend, my friend! You're like Margot Robbie!"

"Pffft. Please. She's a hack," she laughed. Her laugh was like a little child's. It took over her whole body, and the sound of it fluttered in the treetops and echoed off the hills.

"It's so good to see you, babe. I missed you so much."

"What're you doing, girl? Oh my god! You're getting married!"

"Can you believe it?"

"I can. I can absolutely believe it. You're an amazing woman. And Dave's ok."

Katie laughed.

"Naw. JK. Dave's cool. There was a time back in like sixth grade. Back when you guys weren't dating yet. You were just (air quotes) best friends. I actually asked him to go get pizza with me."

"You did? What?"

"Yeah. But then I realized he's not funny."

Katie laughed. "You're right. He's like not funny at all."

"No. He's like as funny as a doorknob."

"I think you mean door nail."

"No. I think actually a door nail is funnier than Dave. Because come on, like, what the heck's a door nail? It's not even really a thing. That's funnier than Dave's ever been in his whole life."

"Actually, I think it's deader than a door nail."

"Well, a door nail's definitely dead."

"Now, in Dave's defense. He was pretty funny when we were in elementary school."

"That's a terrible defense, darling," Chloe said, slipping back into her British accent. "That was like 16 years ago. He hasn't been funny in almost two decades."

"So did you guys get pizza?"

"Heck no! I need someone who's gonna make me laugh. Once I realized that. I was like nuh-uh, Dave. I don't care how sweet and kind and lovable you are. I don't care that you're gonna be a great hubby and dad some day and a great provider and a beautiful singer with pipes of gold and the spirit of God in your fingers when you play guitar. You ain't funny. You ain't my dude."

"So what? You like rescinded your pizza offer?"

"Rescinded it! I told him my dad was making me cut the grass, so I couldn't go."

"What? Are you serious? How did I not know about this years ago?"

"Cuz I just made it up."

"What?"

"I made it up. I didn't ask him out, girl. Are you kidding me? Everybody knew he was your dude. Since Kindergarten. Day one. This day, your wedding day, has been predestined! Listen to me, girl. Since the dawn of time itself. Since God saw the waters and spoke Creation into being, your wedding day with this man has been waiting. Waiting. Like a rock in the center of the earth. Like hot magma waiting in a crevice to erupt from the volcano of time and fill you with his sperm and give you his babies. "

"What? What are you talking about? You just made it so freakin' weird! I mean, that started out like kind of nice. And then it just got so weird."

"I know, right? I been working on my weirdness. I think it looks good on me."

"It totally does."

Chloe was dressed in a simple, black and white Howling Run Center of the Arts hoodie and blue jeans. Her hair was pulled back in a ponytail. She wasn't wearing any make-up. She never did. Her eyes were striking. Her eyes were windows. They were large and expressive and bright. Like two drops of water hanging, quivering, suspended in time, and reflecting everything from the world around them.

"Uh," Chloe said. "Why is there blood in the backseat of your dad's car?"

"Oh no. I completely forgot it."

"You forgot that you murdered someone? And dumped the body in the reservoir?"

Katie laughed. "No. Dave slipped on the ice last night and hit his head on the walkway."

"Holy nuts! But he's ok?"

"Yeah. He has a concussion. But that's why I texted you. I need you, Chloe. He's out of commission for the next three days, and I need your help to get things ready for the wedding."

"Well, you know I'm your girl, boo. But first things first. We gotta get this blood out your dad's car. We can't have him driving 'round town, people thinking he murdered a body. That ain't a good look for a man of God."

So they got some rubber gloves and soap and water, and they scrubbed until it was a pink swirl. Then they finished it off with bleach, and it was good as new. Then, they wound down the windows to air the car out, because the smell was making them dizzy.

"Ok. Next thing we need to do is decorate," Katie said. "The church is open. We can get in there any time."

"Let's do it!"

They jumped in Chloe's Jeep and drove to Dave's house. The trailer with the Christmas tree was still hooked up to Dave's Mazda. Chloe knew exactly how to disconnect the trailer. Then, she and Katie pushed it down a slight slope beside the driveway until she could back her Jeep up to it and hook it up.

They knocked on Dave's door, and his brother, Jonah, answered.

"Hey, Jonah," said Katie.

"What's up, freak?" Chloe gave him a fist bump.

"How's Dave doing?"

Jonah shrugged. He turned and walked away.

"Good to see you too, bro," Chloe quipped.

The girls went up into the attic, where Katie knew all of Dave's Grandma's Christmas ornaments were stored. When they got up there, it was a Christmas wonderland. There were bins and bins and boxes and boxes of ornaments. There were trees and wreaths and garlands. Reindeers. And so many nativity sets. Katie picked her favorite nativities, and they loaded them into the Jeep. Then, they made trip after trip loading in the ornaments.

On their last trip, they ran into Maggie.

"Hey, Maggie."

"Hi Katie. Chloe. Good to see you."

"How's Dave?"

"He's doing ok. He's awake and alert and everything. But he's just lying around in the dark, doing nothing. He's pretty down in the dumps."

"Can we go see him?"

"Uh. Let me go check on him. He's been sleeping a lot. Be right back."

~

There was a gentle, almost silent knock at the door. Dave heard it, but didn't say anything. The door creaked slowly open, and a spray of light from the hallway slashed across the floor and up along the far wall.

"David?" It was barely even a whisper. "Are you awake?"

"Mom. You don't have to whisper. I'm fine. You can talk to me like a normal person."

"Sorry, Davey. Katie and Chloe are here to see you."

"No. Mom. I can't right now."

"What? What do you mean? Why not?"

"I just can't talk to her right now."

"David. She's gonna be your wife in four days. She wants to know how you're doing. You need to talk to her."

"Just tell her I'm doing fine. Tell her I'm sleeping."

"I'm not gonna lie to your fiancée for you. We raised you better than this, David. You need to talk to her."

"No. Mom. Not right now. I'll call her later."

"Promise me you'll call her later."

"I promise, mom. Just leave me alone. Please."

"David. You're a grown man. But you're acting like a teenager. You need to get over this right quick or I'll be growling at you. I expect this kind of behavior from Jonah and Luke. But not from you."

Maggie walked into the hallway where Katie and Chloe were waiting.

"Sorry, girls. He's resting right now. Can you come back later?"

"Is he ok?"

"Yeah. Yeah. He's fine," she smiled broadly. "He just needs to get some rest right now."

"Ok. Well. We'll come by again later."

"That sounds great. So good to see you too. We can't wait for the wedding."

~

Katie shut the door of the Jeep and buckled her seat belt.

"I think Dave's mad at me," she said.

"What? How could he be mad at you? You're perfect."

"I don't know about that." She breathed out deeply. "I'm going through something pretty big right now. And I finally told him about it on Saturday. And things just haven't been quite the same between us."

"What is it? What're you going through?"

"Well . . . it's hard to explain. I guess the buzz word right now for it is deconstructing."

"Deconstructing? That sounds fun."

"You haven't heard this term?"

"No."

"It's all over the internet. I'm deconstructing my faith. I'm questioning the faith I was raised with, and I'm sort of searching for a faith that is a better fit for who I'm becoming."

"That sounds heavy."

"It is. It's really heavy."

"And Dave's not into it?"

"No. And I get it, because he's gonna be starting his ministry. He got this great new job as a worship pastor, and we're gonna be moving out there to Ohio in, like, a month. And he needs me to support him. We have to be on the same page together."

"Well, being on the same page doesn't have to mean that you guys agree on everything. You know. You can have unity without uniformity."

Katie shrugged. "I guess so."

"Honestly," Chloe said, "I think you guys are thinking way too much about this. Jesus came to give us freedom. Freedom! He doesn't want us to feel trapped and conflicted and confused. He came so we could live life to the fullest. You gotta just live your best life, baby! Let's go! Let's listen to some tunes!"

Chloe pulled out her cell phone and searched for the right playlist. But she only had a few seconds to look, so she picked the first song that seemed upbeat enough. She picked "We Were Owls" by Lovedrug. Which wasn't necessarily a bad choice, but she was hoping they could both sing along to, and who on earth knows any of the lyrics to a Lovedrug song. Chloe was startlingly good at many things, but choosing a song to fit the moment wasn't one of them. She absolutely loved music, but she connected to songs for unique reasons that may not make sense to everybody.

Anyway, even though it was an excellent song, it ultimately fell flat in the moment as they drove to the church. When the song ended, the playlist automatically skipped to a random song, and it happened to land on "Physician Heal Thyself" by Zao, a metalcore/post-hardcore band from Greensburg, PA. There were apocalyptic drums and cataclysmic guitars and scary, screaming vocals.

"What is this," Katie asked. And they both just burst out laughing. "You actually listen to this?"

Chloe started screaming along to the music. Her voice rattled and barked and snarled. It matched every syllable of the song perfectly.

"Oh my god, no," said Katie. "Stop it. Stop that right now. That's disgusting."

Chloe kept right on screaming.

"How are you even doing that with your voice? It's, like, terrifying how good you are at that. Stop it."

Chloe burst out laughing. And then Katie joined her. If it wasn't for their seatbelts, they would have both fallen out of their seats onto the floor.

∾

When they arrived at the church, they pulled out the Christmas trees, carried them inside, and found just the right place for each one. Two in the sanctuary and the rest in the reception hall. They got water from the sink in the bathroom and fill all the bases. Then, they got out all the bins and boxes of bulbs and ornaments and started decorating. They worked straight through lunch and didn't even notice.

"You seeing anybody," Katie asked out of the blue, while they hung bulbs.

Chloe shrugged. "Nah. Been too busy. And boys're gross anyways."

"I thought maybe you'd be dating a celebrity now, like, Orlando Bloom or something," Katie smiled.

"Orlando Bloom? When's the last time you saw a movie?"

"Been a while. So what've you been up to?"

Chloe's lips frowned almost imperceptibly, but Katie noticed. "Uh. Well, I just bought some land around here, actually. You know the old Peterman Farm?"

"Yeah."

"His grandkids sold off 68 acres, over half the farm. It hadn't been farmed in decades. Just growing over, and they needed the money."

"So you're a farmer then?"

Chloe smiled. "Yeah. I hope to be. Actually just got back from a three-week course at the Rodale Institute over in Kutztown. Learned about some organic farming practices."

"Are you serious?"

"Yeah. You know the food we eat today is garbage. We've ruined the soil, zapped out all the nutrients, so there's no nutrients in the produce we grow. So we're not getting the nutrition we need. And that's why there's so many more chronic health problems than there ever were before."

"What?"

"Yeah. It's crazy. So I'm learning to restore the earth, to be a good steward of the soil so the nutrients'll return, and humanity won't die off in a hundred years."

"Dear God. You're a superhero!"

"I know."

Katie's phone buzzed. She thought it was Dave, so she snatched it up and answered, "Hello."

"Hey, Katie." It was Gideon.

"Oh. Hey, Giddy. What's up?"

"Hey. I heard about what happened to our boy. Sucks."

"I know. He's gonna be ok, though. Doctor says he's as good as could be expected. He just needs rest. And he can't injure his brain again before it fully heals. It could actually be life-threatening."

"Yeah. Hey. I decided to change my plans for the Batch party. I feel bad, 'cuz I legit had the most epic party planned you could imagine. It was gonna be legendary, and we were all gonna come home with concussions . . ."

"Oh. Well. That's . . ."

"But given his situation, I decided to keep it more low key."

"Good."

"We're just gonna chill at my place tomorrow night for the Steelers game. They're playing a Thursday Night Game this week. I'm brewing some root beer in my basement. We'll just hang in my man cave and watch the game and eat junk food and drink my homebrewed root shine."

"I think that sounds perfect."

"Yeah. Hey, could you bring over that homemade pizza you make? Maybe around 6:30 on Thursday?"

"Yeah. Sure."

"Thanks, Katie. I'm just really bummed about our boy."

"I know, Gid. Me too."

"Thanks for taking such good care of him."

"Sure, dude," she told him.

"Bye."

She hung up and put the phone in her back pocket. She turned to Chloe.

"That was Giddy."

"Who's Giddy?"

"Gideon from high school."

Chloe shook her head.

"Football player. Big, dumb jock. He used to swear with insect words. Like holy horseflies! Or . . . what the beetles!?"

"Oh yeah. I remember that guy. You still talk to him?"

"He's, like, Dave's best friend."

"Really?"

"Yeah. He's actually a pretty good guy underneath all the bravado and crassness."

"Really?"

Katie nodded with a grin. "He wants me to make my homemade pizza for the bachelor party. I don't remember ever making homemade pizza."

"Girl, I love you. You've never made homemade anything."

"I know. I . . ."

"I got you, babe."

"You can make homemade pizza?"

"Yeah," she shrugged. "Howling Run had a baking workshop one time, long time ago. It's not hard. Just takes time. You gotta plan it out. Your mom got a pizza stone?"

Katie shook her head.

"That's alright. I got you."

⁓

Dave was still lying alone in the dark in his bed. He had to pee, but he refused to get up. There was a streak of light glowing in under the door. He could hear water rushing through the pipes in the walls.

He closed his eyes and had a vision of himself as an old man. Tired. Alone. Sad. A ragged hole in his slippers. A sinkful of unwashed dishes. Every time he closed his eyes, he saw another vision from his dream last night while he was unconscious. He was afraid to close his eyes.

⁓

It was almost dinner time. Katie and Chloe had finished decorating the last Christmas tree, and they were setting up a vintage electric train set they had found in Dave's attic. There were enough tracks to go all the way around the reception hall, but they were having trouble getting the train engine to run.

"Are you guys going on a honeymoon," Chloe asked.

"Chloe. At this point, I'm not even sure he still wants to marry me."

Chloe came over and wrapped her arms around her. "Of course he does. You guys were made for each other. And that boy loves you more than you can imagine. More than anyone has ever loved me. I see it in his face when you're with him. He's head over heels."

Katie buried her face in Chloe's shoulder and sobbed. Chloe pushed out of the hug and put her hands on Katie's shoulders. She wiped her tears away. She looked dead into her eyes. She smiled and said, "Boy had a traumatic head injury last night. Let's give him a couple days. And it'll be right as rain."

Katie nodded. Chloe hugged her again.

After fixing the train set, they jumped in Chloe's Jeep and headed back to Katie's house for dinner. They made some rigatoni and sat on the couch in the living room and ate while Katie's dad's toy train hummed through the room.

"Chloe," Katie said.

"Yeah?"

"You remember when you lived with us for a few months after your dad moved to Pittsburgh?"

"Of course."

"Remember when we would lie awake at night and talk."

"Yeah. And it was so cold in your room, I would put on all the clothes I owned and my warmest, fuzziest socks."

"Yeah. And we'd both get in my bed together under the covers to stay warm. And I'd turn the flashlight on under the blankets, and we'd tell stories and read magazines together. Or listen to music on my ipod. Remember ipods?"

"I miss those times."

"Me too."

Katie convinced Chloe to spend the night in her room for old times' sake. She walked with Chloe out to her Jeep. It was so much colder than it had been earlier. After the sun went down, the temperature had plummeted. Chloe grabbed a backpack and sleeping bag out of her trunk, and they ran back into the house. By the time they got to the porch, Katie put it together that Chloe was basically living out of her car.

While Chloe was taking a shower, Katie texted Dave: "How are you?" Then, she put her phone away. She pulled on a sweater. The cold was sneaking in through the walls.

～

Dave was cold. He could feel the temperature dropping. The wood frame of the house started popping and cracking as cold warped the boards and shifted them against the nails that held them in place. At first, he thought it was gunfire. And for a moment, he welcomed the end. He imagined bullets breaking in through his headboard and tearing into his skin.

The sound of another board popping startled him back to reality. He pulled the blanket up to his chin and shivered. He blinked and saw another fractured image from his dream. He couldn't quite tell what it was a picture of, but it left him feeling hopelessly alone and afraid.

And he hated Katie. Hated her. What did he hate her for? For tricking him. For making him think he could ever have a happy life with her. For making him feel hope for their future. And then for ripping it all away from him and leaving him empty and alone. And lost. The darkness crept in around him.

"I wish my suffering could be weighed and my misery put on scales. My sadness would outweigh all the sand of the seas." It was a line from the book of Job that he had always remembered. "The arrows of the Almighty are in me. My spirit drinks in their poison. God's terrors are gathered against me." He remembered those words, because they seemed silly to him when he read them the first time years ago. But now he knew better. Those words are life. They were his life. Those words were his life. He felt them deep in his heart. He was afraid.

～

Katie was still slightly wet from her shower when she walked up the stairs to her room. Chloe was on the floor in a sleeping bag. She had taken a pillow from Katie's dresser drawer.

She stepped over Chloe and crawled under the covers on her bed. She looked up into the dark at a patch of light on the ceiling, streaming in through the window.

"Good night, Chloe."

"Good night. So tired."

"I love you."

"Love you too."

Katie didn't think that everything was going to be right as rain. She had a bad feeling. She felt it like a spider feels the web tingling under its feet. Things were not ok between her and Dave. It wasn't just the concussion. He was pulling away.

Chapter 5

Wednesday

Wednesday was a blur of a day for everybody. Katie and Chloe ate Fruit Loops for breakfast. They drove in Chloe's Jeep at breakneck speed to Walmart and bought some more decorations, some tablecloths. They picked up some antique vases for the reception centerpieces at Mrs. Ringbloom's house. Mrs. Ringbloom had been a member of Katie's church for sixty years. She had known Katie since she was a little girl. She had a collection of vintage vases, and she wanted Katie to use them for her wedding. When they got there, Mrs. Ringbloom had them all packaged up in boxes with old newspaper wrapped around them. She fed Katie and Chloe fresh-baked chocolate chunk cookies and gave them some matcha tea. Before they left, she wrapped the remaining cookies in a cloth napkin and gave them to Katie. Katie felt her boney fingers and scratchy nails. Mrs. Ringbloom smiled at her and then she winked at Chloe.

After Mrs. Ringbloom's, they drove to the church and started decorating. Within an hour, Maggie showed up. A little later, Katie's parents came. Katie's dad dragged the old ladder out of the church basement and started stringing Christmas lights up in the rafters above the sanctuary.

At lunchtime, Maggie pulled some lunch meat sandwiches out of a cooler. They all ate in the wooden pews, which creaked every time someone moved.

∼

There was a knock at Dave's door. It was a soft knock, but he could tell it wasn't his mom just by the sound of it. He thought it must be Luke or Jonah.

"What?"

The door creaked open, and Gideon walked in slowly, gently. Sneaking in along the walls. "What's up, bro?"

"Hey, Giddy."

"How ya feelin'?"

Dave blinked and swallowed. "I'm alright."

"You scared me, bro."

"I think I scared myself."

"You're my dude, you know?"

"I know."

"Anything I can do for you?"

"No. I'm good."

"You need water or something to eat?"

"No."

Gideon noticed a water bottle on the nightstand by his bed. He grabbed it and handed it to Dave.

"Thank you." Dave took a very long drink.

"Just sittin' here in the dark, huh?"

"Yeah. Light's hard on my eyes. Gives me a headache."

"That sucks, man."

"Yeah."

Gideon pulled up a chair and sat next to Dave. He sat there for a long time. They didn't say anything. They just breathed in and out. Before he left an hour later, he got Dave two more bottles of water from the fridge and set them on the nightstand.

"See you, bro."

"Thanks for stopping by."

"Love you, dude."

"Love you too, man."

~

The crew decorated the church all afternoon. Around dinnertime, they called it a night and drove home. When Chloe pulled her Jeep into Katie's driveway, there was a rusted, beat-down, faded green pickup truck in the yard they didn't recognize.

After they parked under the willow tree, Katie's parents met them out in the driveway.

"Katie," her dad started. "We love you, sweetie." He kissed her on the forehead.

"Love you too."

"We know you're gonna be moving out soon. On to your great adventure! The journey of a lifetime. And we couldn't be happier or more proud of you. But we know that you need a car. You've needed one for a very long time. So this bag of bolts over here is yours if you want it."

"Really?! Omigosh. Thank you so much! I can't believe it! It's perfect!"

Her dad handed her the keys, and she jumped up into the driver's seat. She started it up and cranked down the window. Her dad came over, leaned on the truck, and poked his head in through the open window.

"Where'd you get this," she asked.

"From Floyd." Floyd Kayweather was a longtime member of the church who owned a shady auto shop out of his garage. "Gave us a handsome deal."

"Thank you, Daddy!"

Katie took a picture of the truck on her phone and texted it to Dave with the caption: "my new ride."

~

Dave finally got up and went to the bathroom. It was dark. He had no idea what time it was. He went downstairs and pulled a fresh bag of kettle-cooked potato chips out of the kitchen cupboard. He started snacking and walking around the house from room to room, leaving a trail of chip dust. He had no destination, but his appetite was finally returning, and his legs didn't feel quite so rickety.

After he devoured half the chips, he dropped the bag on the couch and went back to bed. He pulled out his phone and called Katie.

~

Katie was lying in bed. Chloe was snoring softly in her sleeping bag on the floor. Katie was exhausted but just couldn't sleep. She kept seeing Dave in her mind—a picture of him lying unconscious on the ground. And for that one moment, she didn't know if he was alive or dead.

Her phone buzzed. It was Dave. She answered.

"Hello."

"Hi."

There was a long silence between them.

"How are you," she finally asked.

"I'm feeling a little better, I think."

"That's great." She strained to sound hopeful and excited, but she failed.

"Katie." He swallowed. "I just don't know . . ."

"What?"

"I don't know if I can do this."

"Do what?"

"I don't know if I can move forward with us like this. We're too different now. Like all of a sudden. How are we gonna do ministry together if we can't agree? How're we gonna raise our kids? How is this gonna work?"

She was crying. "I don't know the answers. But I believe in us. I truly, deep down in my bones, David. I believe that we can make it work. We can serve each other. Support each other. Every couple disagrees. No two people on earth agree on everything. God didn't make us the same. He made us different. We complement each other. Our kids will need both of us. Both ideas. Both perspectives."

"I don't know, Katie. I can't see it right now."

"David, please . . ." Her tears were flowing. She couldn't say anything else. She was gasping for air.

"Katie. This isn't like that. I'm not saying we should call off the wedding or anything. I just . . . this is hard. And I need a minute to think. I need some space for a bit."

"What," she gasped. "I don't . . . understand."

"I don't either. That's the best I can do right now. I gotta go now. I'm feeling a little woozy."

He hung up.

She was sobbing. Her body was shaking. Chloe came over, sat on the bed beside her, and gave her a hug. They stayed like that for ten minutes. Eventually, Katie exhausted herself from the crying, and she fell asleep sitting up. Chloe gently laid her down on her pillow and tucked her in.

~

Dave was feeling nauseous. He did want to call off the wedding. He just didn't have the heart to tell Katie. How could he possibly tell her? She was the love of his life. He would never find anyone else like her. He would wind up alone and sad. And that certainly wasn't what he wanted either.

He laid in bed, gazing up at a splash of moonlight on the ceiling. His eyes felt heavier, and as he was drifting off to sleep, he thought of John the Baptist living out in the wilderness. Unwashed. Unshaven. Wearing a camel hair vest with a leather belt. Eating locusts and wild honey stolen from beehives. But he was a voice crying out in the wilderness. Maybe that would be Dave's destiny. Maybe that was his calling. Sad and alone. But a voice crying out in the wilderness. That didn't sound so bad. Right before he fell asleep, he remembered that John the Baptist was murdered around age 30.

He woke up to the sound of gunfire popping again in their walls as the temperature continued to drop. He was left with a vision from his dream of Katie. She was old and alone. Her hair was gray. Her face was wrinkled and leathery. She was sitting in a rocking chair, knitting a pair of wool socks. He realized they were both doomed to be sad and alone.

"What's the point," he said out loud. Outside, the wind whistled. Tree branches scraped against the shingles. The wooden frame of the house twisted with loud pops and bangs.

"Please, God," he prayed. "I don't want to be alone. I don't want Katie to be alone."

He had to tell her.

Chapter 6

Thursday

KATIE WOKE UP ON Thursday morning with a tightly-wound knot in her chest and a deep desire that things could be different. Her whole body felt heavy, like her bones were made of stones, as she rose from the bed. She forgot where she was on her way down the steps. She couldn't remember where she was going. If she was even going anywhere.

At the bottom of the steps, she heard her mom's rocking chair creaking. She turned to go into the living room, and she saw Chloe sitting there beside her mom. They were both knitting.

Chloe looked up. "Your mom's teaching me how to knit." She smiled.

Her mom smiled. "She's a natural." She reached out and tapped Chloe's knee and smiled at her.

After breakfast, Katie and Chloe jumped in Katie's new truck, and they drove into Punxsutawney to pick up their bridal dresses at Lia's Bridal and Tuxedo.

"I can't believe how slow you drive," Chloe told her.

"Ok, now shut up, because you drive like a total freak job, and I have never once complained about it in all these years."

Chloe put her hands up. "Ok. Alright. I'm just saying. Your wedding will be over, and you'll be on your honeymoon by the time we get there."

"Shut up!"

For a while, they drove in silence. Then, Chloe put her hand on Katie's shoulder, and Katie immediately started crying.

"Hey. That boy loves you. He loves the stars outta you. He just needs a minute. Everything's gonna be right as rain. I promise."

~

When they got to Lia's Bridal Shop, there was no parking in the lot, so they drove around the block six times, because Katie was afraid to parallel park on the street. Eventually, she just decided to park at the McDonald's across the street, and they walked over.

Everyone at the bridal shop was so friendly, but Katie was dying inside, and she looked a wreck. All the other brides-to-be were beaming and radiant, and shehad snot bubbles. She decided not to try on the dress at the store, even though Chloe told her she should. She just didn't want to. And it was Chloe who realized that they should pick up the tuxedos too, because Dave wasn't able to make the drive. So they left the store completely weighed down with clothes. Arms full. They scurried across the street like worker ants loaded down with bread crumbs.

When they got back to Katie's house, Chloe convinced her to try on the wedding dress, and she offered to take the tuxedos over to Dave's house.

"Ok," was all Katie could think to say.

In a flash, Chloe tossed all the tuxes, still wrapped in plastic into the back seat of her Jeep. Her tires kicked up gravel as she pulled down the driveway.

She didn't knock at Dave's house. She just walked right in the front door. She stomped up the steps with all the tuxes in her arms, and she burst into Dave's bedroom. It was dark except for a jagged ray of sunlight through the blinds. She dropped the tuxes on the floor and stormed over beside his bed. She walked directly to her mark and stopped cold. She delivered her line clearly and with conviction.

Chloe: "You little jerk."

Dave: "Chloe?"

Chloe: "I know you know how special Katie is. She is the love of your life. And you're a complete idiot."

Dave: "Why're you here?"

Chloe: "If you weren't such an idiot, I wouldn't have to be here. But you're leaving me no choice. You're about to make the biggest mistake of your pathetic, little life."

Dave: "What are you talking about?"

Chloe: "You freakin' know what I'm talking about."

Dave: "Do you know she just dumped that on me one week before our wedding?"

Chloe: "You need to be a man and grow a pair right now. You need to get over this dark night of the soul bit you got going on here and do the right thing. This is your chance. And I gotta tell you. You're blowing it right now. Katie is a goddess. You have no idea how tender her heart is. She is your best chance at living a life filled with love and joy and beauty. And you know it."

Dave: "I just don't know if that's true anymore."

Chloe: "That's trash, David. You're just scared. And it's ok to be scared. This is a huge moment. Like maybe the hugest moment in your life. But you gotta step up now, bro, or you're gonna regret it for the rest of your life. If you don't call her by the time I get back over there, I'm gonna come right back here and kick your teeth in."

Chloe exits.

~

Katie cried while trying on her dress. She had the dress on, but she was on the floor. It looked like there was nobody in it at all, just a dress puddled on the floor, except for one, naked foot peeking out.

Her phone buzzed. She snatched it up.

"Hello?"

"Hey."

She sat up like a bolt. "Hi."

"I love you, Katie. You know I do."

"I love you too."

"I feel tight right now. Like stuck. You know?"

"Mmm-hmm."

"I don't feel like I'm thinking very clearly."

"Ok."

"I want you to know that I love you, and I want to marry you. But can we just, like. Can you just give me, like, a little time?"

"You need time?"

"I just need to clear my head. Some time."

"David, our wedding is like three days away. I can't do this. I can't feel this for another three days. We can't be all, like, up in the air like this."

"I'm not. Katie, you can't make it seem like this is all on me. It's not. You could've told me months ago. I could've processed this already."

"Well. Do you wanna call off the wedding."

"No. I don't. I just need to think, Katie. I can't think. I don't know where God is, but He's not here. Not here with me right now. I'm on my own."

"You don't have to be alone. I'm right here. I'll come over in a heartbeat if you want me."

"Not. Now. Not yet."

"I understand."

"Thank you. I love you."

"Love you too."

She hung up.

Chloe came up the stairs and found a wedding dress puddle with a naked foot peeking out.

"You ok?"

"I messed up."

"You didn't mess up. You were honest with your fiancée. You did the right thing. Now, it's his turn to do the right thing."

"Ok." She didn't move. She stayed a puddle.

After lunch, they started working on the homemade pizzas. First, they went to Mackey Grocers and got all the ingredients. Next, they stopped by Howling Run Center for the Arts and picked up two big pizza stones. Then, they went back to Katie's house and started working in the kitchen. There was no recipe. Chloe was just making magic.

She used a ton of butter and explained that it was the secret to making the best pizza dough. Katie was skeptical but went along for the ride. They made two separate batches of dough and put them in bowls. They covered them with cloth napkins and set them out to rise in her dad's library.

Then, they sat and ate Mrs. Ringbloom's cookies.

"Did I tell you where we're going for your bachelorette party?"

"I don't want a party," Katie groaned.

"Eck!"

"What?"

"Eck! That's lame. We're gonna celebrate you!"

"I don't. . ."

"Shoosh! After we drop off the pizzas at Gideon's, we're gonna go to Rainmaker Lodge."

"I just don't. . ."

"Shoosh! We're gonna have a nice meal. We're gonna look out the picture window and watch all the rich people ski. We're gonna listen to some live music. We're gonna eat cheesecake. We're gonna sample some wine. Or drink apple juice."

"They do have good apple juice there."

"And we're just gonna let all the junk flow off our backs like water. And we're just gonna forget that anything exists except the joy of the moment that is right in front of us."

~

Gideon drove his F-150 and picked up Dave. He took them back to his place. The truck bounced Dave around and made him feel sick. When they got to Gid's rutted driveway, Dave thought for a second he was going to throw up. But then, suddenly, he felt better.

He got out of the truck and walked down by the lake. The sun was setting in a dramatic splash of red and gold across the sky. He pulled up his hood against the cold and skipped a rock. Even though it was cold, it felt good to be outside.

"Bro," Gideon began. "You and Katie have the talk?"

"We been talking and talking and talking."

"Yo, man. She's good people. No doubt, but I'm worried 'bout you. I don't see how it's gonna work with you two anymore. It's been keeping me up at night, actually."

"Really?"

"Yeah, man." A fresh, tiny tear popped in his eyes. He slashed it away with the back of his hand. "You my boy. I love you, man." He clapped his hand on Dave's shoulder, and they hugged. "But I know you love her. I do. I see it. So I get what you're going through. You know? And you gotta do whatever God is leading. Whatever God puts in your heart. Can I pray with you?"

"Oh. Yeah. For sure, man."

Gid placed his arm across Dave's back and his hand on his far shoulder. He bowed his head and raised his hand to the sky. "Lord God. My boy Dave here is your anointed one. You have called him out to fight the lions and to face the giants of this world. You have placed a calling in his heart to live a life set apart for You. And I pray right now, Father, for peace in his soul. And in his body. And in his spirit. Because right now, Father, there are slings and arrows. There is unrest in his soul, Lord God. You are putting him through this trial so that he may be made complete and fully equipped for the life You have called him to live. But right now, Father, he needs your light. He needs your lamp unto his feet. Your light unto his path. Give him clear direction, Lord. Guide him. Lead him. Brighten his path, Father. Send your pillar of fire to light his way in this darkness. Help him to lean on you, as you know he will. Give him peace in this moment. We love you, Father. In your name. Amen."

Gideon wiped another tear from his face. He gave Dave a hug. "I love you, brother," he told him.

"Love you, too, Gid."

"Now let's go drink some root beer and eat Doritos and see if we can burp loud enough the neighbors'll hear us."

Gideon led Dave down into his basement. He showed him his root beer brewing system. He handed him a glass jug full.

"This is yours, bro! I call it Root Shine."

There was even a black label on the jug that said, "Root Shine" in gold letters.

Dave plopped down on the couch and plucked the cork from the glass jug. He took a swig, and he saw that it was good. It was very good. It was sweet, but it had a kick too. He drank some more.

Gideon turned on the tv, which had a huge 75-inch screen, and he flipped the channel to the pregame coverage for the Steelers game. Then, he plopped down on the couch, put his feet up on the coffee table, popped the corked of his own jug of Root Shine and took a drink. He opened a bag of Doritos. And to Dave's surprise, they actually did drink root beer, eat Doritos, and burp.

Gideon turned up the volume to show off his sound system. The sound of the broadcast filled up the whole room. Dave could hear the crowd of fans in the background. He heard a woman shouting, and it sounded like she was right behind them. He had never heard audio quite as immersive.

"Had Bose come in all the way from Grove City to design a custom system for the man cave," Gid told him.

"Ok."

"I know. It's awesome." Gideon smiled at him like a little kid.

"It's, like, actually kind of creepy how good the sound is."

"I know!"

About twenty minutes later, Luke and Jonah showed up. They didn't ring the doorbell. They just came on in and down the stairs.

"We heard you guys burping when we were coming down the driveway," said Jonah. "And I told Luke, we have come to the right place." The twins laughed together.

As the coin toss was happening on the screen, Katie and Chloe came down the stairs carrying two huge pizzas, fresh out of the oven.

"Hey, boys," said Chloe.

"Your man cave delivery service," Katie piped in.

They placed the pizzas on the wood coffee table.

"What's that smell," Chloe asked, and everybody shrugged.

Gideon leaned over to Dave and whispered, "Who is that?"

"Who, Chloe? You know Chloe."

Gideon shook his head slowly. "She's. . ."

"I know, dude. She's gorgeous. Put your tongue back in your head."

"You mean, like, Chloe from ninth grade?"

"Yeah."

Gideon looked her up and down in our skinny jeans and flannel shirt with her hair pulled back into a tight braid. He stood up. "I'm Gideon," he told her.

"Yeah. I remember you," Chloe told him.

"Yeah. I mean. Sure. I remember you too. Been a long time."

Chloe nodded. "You still a jerk?"

"Pretty much."

"Ok."

"But I'm working on it."

"Well, good for you."

"You went to boarding school, right?"

"I went to the Linden School in Wheeling. In their theater program."

"Cool. Cool."

"Hated every second of it, but it helped me get where I wanted to be. So . . ." She shrugged. "What do you do?"

"Oh. Uh. I own my own tree business."

"Ok."

"I got a small bee farm I'm working on."

"Yeah. We saw the beekeeper suit hanging up by your front door. Kinda creepy, dude."

"I know. Pretty dope, right!"

"Not really."

"Chloe's getting into farming too," Katie said. "She just bought like 60 acres and took a course on organic farming practices. She's gonna save the world."

"Really? That's awesome," Gideon said.

"Oh gentle knights," Chloe said with a British flourish and a sweeping gesture that filled the room. "We shall now bid you adieu. And leave you to your noble pursuits."

"Wait," said Gideon. "Before you go, take a bottle of Root Shine. I made it myself." He handed her a jug.

"Thank you?"

Chloe and Katie disappeared up the stairs. Katie looked back at Dave. Their eyes collided for a long moment, but there was nothing communicated discernibly in their expressions. Then, she turned and left.

She jumped in Chloe's Jeep. The car doors clapped shut.

"I think he likes you," Katie said.

"Who? Knucklehead?"

"Yes. I mean, I'm talking about Gideon, and I assume that's who you mean by knucklehead."

Chloe cranked the key and turned to look at her. "Yes." She laughed. "He's no Orlando Bloom."

Her Jeep rumbled down the driveway on their way to Rainmaker Lodge, which is just on the other side of Rainmaker Mountain, opposite the cross.

"Do you think women should be able to be pastors," Katie asked as they tore down the road between naked, gray trees.

"Heck no," Chloe quipped. "Don't put that on us. We got enough to do."

"But don't you think that's sexist? We should be able to do anything we set out to do. Anything we want to do."

"Katie. We already make the world go 'round. Don't try to put that on us too."

"Are you serious? How can you believe that? Why would you want to limit us like that? Look at what women are permitted to do in ministry. We just get to do all the stuff the men don't want to do."

"You think that's true?"

"Yes. We do the kids' ministries, because the men don't have the patience for it. We do the cleaning and the secretarial work, because the men can't be bothered."

"Doesn't Dave's mom lead the worship at your church?"

"Yes. But she never gets the credit she deserves."

"So do you think your dad's a sexist?"

"Yes. I do."

Chloe looked over at her. "Katie. You have no idea how good of a man your dad is. Seriously. He took me in when my own dad just couldn't be bothered. I thank God for your dad all the time. Your dad is not sexist."

"Chloe, if you were gay or if you were a drinker or a druggie, he would have left you just be homeless. He would have never taken you in."

"And he would've been right to do it. He would've done it to protect you. My dad couldn't even lift a finger for me. He just sent me away. When he sent me away to Linden, I called him every night that first week, because I hated it so much. And by the third night, he just stopped answering my calls. Those girls were so mean to me. I will never forget the things they said to me, the things they did. And my dad couldn't even pick up the phone."

"I'm sorry, Chloe. That's awful."

"Well. It gave me thick skin. Made me resilient, like a rubber band."

For several minutes, they drove in silence.

"Do you wanna be a pastor," Chloe asked.

"Well, no."

"Then I think you should count your blessings."

"But there are women out there who want to be, who feel called by God into the ministry. If God is calling them, then who are we to say they can't do it."

"That's why I love you, Katie! You're a woman of gentle heart. You're a better person than I'll ever be. Don't listen to me."

"Chloe, shut up! You're an absolutely amazing human being. I look up to you. I aspire to be you."

Chloe let out a little puff of laughter. "No, babe. You don't wanna be me. Trust me."

Chloe's phone started ringing, and she quickly silenced it.

"You're right, Katie. You're absolutely right. You're kind. You care about people. You think about others. And that's the right way to be. But you get that from your parents. Your parents are amazing people, Katie. They're not sexists or bigots. They're salt of the earth people."

Katie didn't say anything. She just looked out the window at the dark trees passing.

Chloe's phone rang again. She turned it off and threw it in the backseat.

"You know what," she said. "I need to stop for a minute." She started pulling the car off the road, and it rumbled in the dirt. Gravel kicked up into the engine.

"What? Here?"

When the car lurched to a stop, Chloe threw the door open and got out. She walked a quick circle around the Jeep. When she passed in front of the headlights, Katie tried to read the expression on her face, but it was a blur. She got out of the car.

"You ok?"

"Yeah. Fine."

Katie could see that she'd been crying. She rushed over and threw her arms around her. Her body was shaking.

"It's ok," Katie said. Chloe cried on her shoulder. After a few minutes, they got back in the car. Katie reached back between the seats and pulled Chloe's phone off the floor in the back. She wiped it off and handed it back to Chloe.

"What'd it ever do to you?"

Chloe gave a little laugh. "It's my agent. She's been calling and calling and calling ever since I got here."

"That's amazing! Chloe, you have to answer her! It has to be good news, right?"

"Well, I told her specifically not to call me until after your wedding. I told her that three times. I told her over the phone. I texted it to her. And I emailed her about it. I told her whatever it is, it can wait until after my best friend gets hitched and rides off into her sunset with her man for her happily ever after."

"But Chloe. It must be really important. You have to answer it."

"I know what it's about."

"You do? What is it?"

"There's this role that I really really wanted, like, nine months ago. I auditioned four times and met with all these people. Some of them were nice. Some of them said some really mean things. Anyway, they decided to go with Millie Bobby Brown."

"Who?"

Chloe turned her eyes at her like screws. "Millie Bobby Brown. Are you kidding me? Do you even watch movies?"

Katie shrugged.

"She was in Stranger Things. Time Magazine's 100 most influential people. It doesn't matter. Anyway, last week, she backed out."

"What? That's amazing! You got the part!"

"But, like, I'm just not sure I want it anymore."

"Why?"

"I don't know, Katie. I don't know if I want this life. It's hard. This role. It's about a woman trying to escape a relationship with her abusive father. And she goes to this prestigious prep school where everyone is mean to her, and then she comes home to this abusive father. And she has no air. Like, she can't breathe. You know? She just has this hope, this dream that she can get into college and leave her old life in the rear view. And I thought, that's me. Like, that's my story. I was born to play this role. Like, that's how I feel every moment of every day."

"It sounds perfect."

"But Katie. I don't want it. I wanna be different. I wanna feel something different. I don't wanna be the girl who's stuck. I wanna be the girl who makes it out. The girl who lives her dream."

"But maybe this role helps you get there. Maybe this really launches your career and changes your life."

"I just don't believe that, Katie. You can't wait on something or someone to swoop into your life like Tarzan and make your dreams come true. That's not how life works. Some role in a stupid movie isn't gonna fix me. I just realized that I gotta do it myself. No one else is gonna do it for me."

Katie reached out and grabbed her hand. Their fingers slipped together. "You don't need to be fixed, Chloe."

"Yes I do."

"Chloe, you're perfect just as you are. God loves you just as you are. You are deeply loved, Chloe. I love you. God loves you. You are a child of the Most High God. You are a woman of wisdom. And strength and dignity. You are strong, Chloe. And beautiful. And one of the best, most loving and courageous people I have ever met. I thank the Lord that I know you. Lord . . . Heavenly Father, your daughter is hurting. Her heart is grieving, and I know that makes your heart grieve too. Pour out a blessing on her, Lord. Pour out a blessing of peace on Chloe right now. Your presence, God. We ask for your presence. Your Holy Spirit to guide us. To guide Chloe. To light up her path. Thank you, God. Father. We turn to you. Our eyes turn to you. Our hearts turn to you. We pray for peace. We pray for healing. May Chloe be restored from the inside out. May she be lifted up into your presence. Lord Jesus. King Jesus. Thank you for your Spirit. Thank you for your love. Thank you for the gift of life in our bodies. For the gift of breath in our lungs. Thank you, Father. Thank you, Jesus. Amen."

Katie let out a deep breath that had been stored up inside of her. She gave Chloe a strong hug. The wind wailed against the car, and Katie heard it for the first time. "I love you, Chloe," she told her.

"Love you too."

～

Dave was mindlessly eating Doritos. He could feel the crunch in his teeth, feel it shooting down along his jawline. The cacophony of flavors burst in his mouth like a 500-person choir erupting suddenly into a single harmonized chord. And each bite rang out a different note. He could hear the sound of the crunching like it was all happening inside his ears. He was chewing so slowly he thought maybe time had slowed down. But he looked at the television screen, and the Steelers game seemed to be moving along at a normal pace.

He took a sudden swig of root beer. The swirling flavors bubbled up in his brain, and he felt a floating sensation, almost like he was leaving the earth. He blinked in slow motion.

Was it the concussion that was making him feel this way? He ate another Dorito, and the sound of the crunching was so loud that he could barely hear the tv. It looked like the Steelers were driving, but it was all confusing.

He wondered what Katie was up to tonight. He wanted her to be here with him on the couch. Slowly, he placed the palm of his hand flat on the couch cushion next to him, hoping that she would somehow be there. But she wasn't.

～

Chloe was driving, fast, through the winding tunnels of trees at Howling Run. She uncorked the jug of Root Shine and took a swig.

"Holy Jehovah! This is good!"

She handed the jug to Katie, who took a long gulp. She exclaimed, "Yeah. Wow! That's good."

"Dude made this in his basement?"

Katie shrugged. "Guess so."

"How many airborne toxins you think made their way into this jug?"

Katie laughed. "That's probably half the flavor."

Chloe's Jeep roared past the entrance to the Howling Run Center Art School. There was a huge, painted, and carved wooden sign arching over a gravel driveway that cuts through a natural grove of cedars. Katie and Chloe both turned their heads to look at it as they drove by.

"What do you think about the LGBTQ community," Katie asked abruptly.

Chloe flashed her a puzzled look. "When did they add the Q?"

"What?"

"What do you mean?"

"I mean, like. Do you think they're all going to hell?"

"I've been around a lot of gay guys in the theater programs I've been a part of. And I'm pretty sure all of those guys are going to hell. For sure."

"What? Why?"

"Well. I guess I'm sort of kidding. But they were all cruel and petty. And they would tear you down in a heartbeat if they thought it would help them get ahead in any way. But. Honestly, that's how everyone was in theater. And at least the gay guys were funny."

"But do you think it's a sin to be gay or transgender or whatever?"

"Katie. I think Christ came to set us free. I just don't think we have to worry about that. It's not our calling in life to figure out who's sinning or who's going to heaven." She shrugged. "That's a waste of time. We're just supposed to live our best life and love the people around us."

"But what if you were gay?"

"Oh, sweetie, I'm definitely not gay."

"I know. But what if you were? You would have to worry about it, because it would be your life."

"But that's my point, Katie. That's not my life. That's not my cross to bear. I can't bear everyone's crosses. I can only bear my own. If I start trying to carry the crosses of every Tom, Dick, and Harry vagina in the world, I'd go crazy."

"But doesn't the Apostle Paul tell us to bear one another's burdens?"

"Who? That guy? Paul was smart and important to the founding of the Christian Church and all that, but he was kind of a douchebag." She laughed. Katie blinked at her. "Ok. Look," Chloe continued. "I think he was probably talking about, like, you and I sharing burdens. Friends. Family. Those closest to you."

"No. He was talking about the church sharing one another's burdens. Sometimes I think Christians exclude people just so they don't have to carry their burdens, because their burdens are hard."

"I don't think Christians back away from hard things."

"Yes they do. They do it all the time. The LGBTQ community wanting to be part of the church complicates their interpretation of Scripture. And that makes them afraid, so they shut down. They run away. They turn against them, so they don't have to face the fact that our faith is complicated and confusing."

"It's not complicated, Katie. Love God. Love others. Those are the commandments. Jesus came to make it simple. To set us free. Our God is not a God of confusion."

"Well. I didn't really mean confusion. I just meant complicated. I think Christians today try to make everything black and white, and that's just not how the world works. Not how God works."

"I just think you're delving into realms where it's not really our place to roam around in."

"What're you talking about?"

"Like. Whoever they are we love them. Gay, straight. Short, tall. Fat, skinny. We love them. Doesn't matter if they're sinning or if they're going to hell. That's not our place. Our place is to love."

"Yeah, but Chloe. Do we let them be Sunday School teachers or deacons or worship leaders in the church? Do we let them lead the congregation?"

"That's just not for me to decide."

"Chloe, you're running away from hard things. This is exactly what I'm talking about."

"You're wrong about that. Christians take responsibility. We hold ourselves accountable right now, because one day we're going to give an account to God. We don't run away. The whole world runs away. Christians stand up."

"And they've taken a stand on the LGBTQ community, and they've shunned them. But not out of conviction. Out of fear."

"Who took a stand? Who are you talking about?"

"Christians. The church."

"What church? Every church should decide for themselves. And it should be about the person. Not because some marginalized (she gives air quotes) group is fighting for power. If they're the right person, then they'll lead. God will make a way. But it shouldn't matter what political group or demographic they happen to identify with."

"But that's not what's happening."

"How do you know?"

"I see it. I have a friend."

"Ariel?"

"Yes. They've been shunned by the church. They were part of the church community and accepted, and then as soon as they came out as gender nonbinary, it was clear they were no longer part of the church family. And it was devastating. It was torture. It's a scar that they'll never forget. That will never fully heal."

"Well, that. Is tragic."

"It is."

"Is Ariel coming tonight?"

"Yes."

"Awesome. Will be great to meet . . . them."

"Who else is coming?"

"Just you, me, Ariel, Letty, and Liz."

"Sweet!"

"Hold onto your butt." Chloe accelerated around a turn and slid off the road for a second before pulling the Jeep back onto the asphalt.

She laughed. Katie shrieked.

"Why would you do that?"

~

Dave took another drink of root beer. He had to pee. He got up and crossed the room. The door to the basement bathroom was wet. He shut the door. He could still hear his brothers belching. He flicked on the light and looked up into the streaked mirror over the sink. Was he crying? It looked like he was. He looked away. He peed. He went back into the room and sat on the couch. The guys didn't even seem to notice that he had been gone. He closed his eyes and tried to sleep.

~

Chloe and Katie were driving almost vertical up Lodge Drive, which winds its way up the side of Rainmaker Mountain to the lodge. Chloe didn't slow down even when it looked like they were about to plummet off the edge of a cliff. It was dark, and the headlights pierced up through the black velvet sky.

They lit up the moon and then wandered around in the dark like a spotlight that can't find the actor on a black stage.

Once they reached the top, they were surprisingly in a giant parking lot filled with cars. Chloe parked.

She glanced a smile at Katie. "You ready?"

"Yeah."

"You're about to get married, baby!"

"It doesn't feel like it."

Chloe reached out and grabbed her arm. "Hey! He's gonna do the right thing. He's a man that does the right thing."

"But what is the right thing?"

"To love you forever."

"I wish things were that simple, Chloe. I do. But . . ."

"But what? It is that simple. He loves you. You love him."

"But how're we gonna raise our kids? Am I gonna be a detriment to his ministry? Are we gonna just keep growing further and further apart and eventually start to resent each other and wish that we'd never even met in the first place?"

"Katie. Stop it! Now who's running away from hard things? Just because something's hard doesn't mean it's wrong. A very wise woman taught me that. Now, let's go eat our faces off and drink whatever we want and play indoor mini golf until we pass out."

They both got out of the Jeep and started walking through the lit parking lot toward the lodge. Chloe checked her phone.

"Letty and Liz aren't coming," she told Katie. "Letty broke her foot. Candy Cane stepped on it."

"Come on, Candy Cane!"

"They're at the hospital now."

"So is Letty gonna be walking down the aisle on crutches?"

She shrugged. "I don't know."

~

"What's up, buddy," Gideon said. "You look like the cat pooped on your lollipop."

Dave blinked. He opened his eyes and turned toward Gideon. "What?"

"What's going on, man? You ok?"

"I don't know, brother. I just can't . . ." His voice trailed off as tears popped and shined in the television light.

Gideon reached out and placed his hand on Dave's shoulder. "I know, bro." Suddenly, he jumped up. "I got an idea. Let's go outside."

"But it's not halftime yet," said Luke.

"It's time, boys. Let's go out."

"But it's cold outside," Jonah complained.

"And dark," Luke added. "And cold."

"I have fireworks," Gideon retaliated.

Luke and Jonah stood up and followed. Gideon knew they were suckers for fireworks. He reached his hand out and helped Dave up from the couch. Dave rolled his eyes, but he got up and followed. They all went outside. Gideon grabbed his hunting rifle and a plastic bag full of fireworks on the way out.

In their coats and boots, they went down to the lake. Gideon pulled a paper boat from behind a tree (who know why it was there). He set it in the water and dumped a bunch of fireworks into it. Then, he pushed the loaded boat out toward the center of the lake.

"We're gonna shoot it," Gideon said.

"That's stupid," Dave chimed in.

"I love it," Jonah shouted. "Can I go first?"

Gideon handed him the rifle. "Wait 'til it gets out further."

Disgusted, Dave looked up at the dark sky. There was a sliver of a moon but no stars anywhere to be seen. He breathed out deep, and a slow, white mist curled up from his body and around the moon.

He sat down on the wet grass with his head between his knees. Luke and Jonah were giggling, but there was no other sound. No frogs. No crickets. No dogs barking across the water. Just a gentle wind, wrapping itself around him. And he thought of the Holy Spirit. The Holy Spirit is wind. He remembered suddenly that the Greek word neuma and the Hebrew word ruach both meant spirit and wind. And breath. He breathed slowly in and out and let the Holy Spirit fill him up. He didn't realize how empty he had felt. But the Spirit was giving him life. The same wind in the branches of the trees was now in his lungs. The same breath from his lungs was now moving the branches and hovering over the waters. Like the Spirit hovering in Genesis 1. In and out. In and out. He breathed.

"It's over."

He heard the words somewhere. Somewhere over the treetops in that dark sky. The words fell down.

"It's over."

And a peace poured over him. When his brother fired the first shot from the rifle, he didn't even notice. Just peace. "It's over."

~

Chloe was sitting on the windowsill of a big, dark picture window, and Katie was sprawled out in a lounge chair. She was locked into her cellphone while sipping a frappuccino slowly through a straw. Chloe checked her phone and then put it back in her pocket.

"What're you doing," Chloe asked.

"I got an idea!"

"Yeah? Tell me about it."

"It's an idea. And I need a playlist. The perfect playlist."

"What's the idea?"

"It's probably a crazy idea."

"Those are the best ones."

"Well . . . for the past week, Dave and I have been basically disagreeing about everything that matters to him. But one thing we don't disagree on is Tozer."

"What's Tozer? Is he, like, a rapper?"

"What? No. Tozer. A.W. Tozer. He was a pastor and writer who died, like, a long time ago. But Dave introduced me to him. He gave me his copy of *The Pursuit of God*. And that book has actually been really helpful for me through this whole process."

"Ok."

"Well, I forgot that Tozer was born around here."

"Where?"

"Newburg."

Chloe shook her head.

"It's like 45 minutes away. And there's a summer camp out there where he spoke many times in the 40's and 50's."

"Ok."

"So I'm gonna pick up Dave tomorrow morning, and we're gonna drive out to Mahaffey camp together. We need an adventure together focused around a shared interest. Something we agree on."

"Uh. Ok."

"You think it's a bad idea."

"No. No. No. I think. It's a great idea."

"I just don't know what else to do, Chloe. I have to fight for us. If our relationship is gonna fall apart, I can't just sit around and wait for him to decide. I have to do everything in my power or I'll regret it for the rest of my life."

Chloe gave her a hug, and Katie cried on her shoulder.

∼

Gideon, Jonah, and Luke all missed on their first shots. It was difficult, because it was so dark. They really couldn't see the paper boat out there on the water. The rifle came back around to Gideon. He peered through the scope and waited for the moonlight to hit the water where it broke against the boat. He saw a little flash, and he fired.

BOOOM!

The sky and the trees shook. Lake water rained down everywhere. A small fire burned out on the lake for several minutes as the paper burned up. They watched the fire intently until it shrunk to an ember that fizzled out in the water.

∼

Katie and Chloe placed their food order, and they sat across the table from each other, under the chandelier.

"Did you call your agent back about that movie?"

Chloe smirked. "Don't be mad at me."

"What?"

"I may have exaggerated my level of angst about that project."

"What do you mean?"

"I mean. I know you, baby, better than you know yourself. You get energy from helping other people. I knew you'd feel better if you could just stop for a moment and help me."

"What?"

"Yeah. I took that role yesterday. I mean I feel a little bit of angst about it. But I'm gonna absolutely crush it. I was born for that role."

"Chloe, you are diabolical. What is wrong with you?"

She shrugged. "You're a good person, Katie. We might disagree on things or whatever, but I love you. And so does David. He knows your heart. He knows exactly how good of a person you are. He sees you."

"I'm not that good."

"You are."

She shook her head. "I sprung this on him, Chloe. I told him one week before our wedding. I should've told him months ago. It's not fair the way I did it to him."

"Listen to me. You're not trying to do anything to him. You're trying to do life with him. You've got be honest with him. Even when it's inconvenient. Even when it hurts. You've got to tell him things that are important to you. Doesn't matter when you told him. You told him."

～

Dave was back on the couch in Gideon's basement. He was grinding his teeth, ready to go home and get to bed. But he didn't want to be disrespectful. The game was still in the third quarter. He squinted at the screen and tried to focus on the score. The Steelers were down by a touchdown, but it looked like they were threatening to score. Inside the ten-yard line.

He closed his eyes, and for a moment, all the angst and confusion of things dissolved away. It was the Spirit. He knew. "The peace of God, which transcends all understanding, will guard your hearts and minds in Christ Jesus." He believed that with his whole heart.

But the world interceded. A stray thought rushed in like a spray of water breaking through a dam. He hadn't really been "single" a day in his life. If he didn't marry Katie, he would have to go start his new job at the church without her. He would just be a single man. A worship pastor at a new church. He couldn't handle that. It would ruin him. It would be a disaster. He didn't want that. It was the last thing he wanted. He would have to decline the job. And then what? He would go to work for his dad? He started crying. He realized that this moment was the end of his life as he knew it. It may seem dramatic, but that was the thought that rushed in and broke his peace wide open and created a flood. He wept.

Then, his cellphone dinged. He sniffled and wiped away some tears and pulled out his phone. A text from Katie: "I'm picking you up tomorrow morning in my new pickup. 11am. Will you go on an adventure with me, poopyface?"

And somehow, a trace of a smile broke through his tears.

～

Katie's phone buzzed. She saw that Dave had responded. It was a very quick response. The quickness of it made her nervous.

"What'd he say," Chloe asked her.

"I don't know."

"Well, read it."

"Ok." She read it silently.

"Read it out loud, goofball."

"Ok. He said, 'I love adventures, squirrelbutt.'"

Chloe jumped out of her seat in the restaurant. "Woooo," she howled. "Look at you two, brave souls."

Katie was crying with joy.

Her phone buzzed again. "Oh shoot." She stood up.

"What?"

"It's Ariel?"

"Who?"

"My friend, Ariel."

"Ok."

"They're lost.

"Who's lost."

"My friend, Ariel."

"They're lost?"

"Yes. They were on their way here, and they got lost."

"Have they heard of Google Maps?"

"Well, they're from the city, and you know how it is around here. Most of the roads don't even have signs. And it's dark."

"Yeah, but the voice literally tells you where to turn."

"We have to go find them?"

"What? Why? Where are they?"

"I don't know." She started texting Ariel back.

"Well. Can we eat our dinner first? I'm starving."

"No, Chloe. They need us."

Katie got up and walked fast for the door with her eyes down at her phone.

"Just text them the address," Chloe yelled after her.

"They have the address."

Chloe pulled out a $100 bill and placed it on the table.

～

The Steelers won on a last-second field goal! Gideon and Dave's brothers were jumping around the room, chest bumping. Dave just watched it all swirl around him.

When it calmed down, he said, "I wanna go home."

Gideon had a mouthful of Doritos. He crunched on them for a few seconds. Then, he said, with one hand curled into a soft fist in front of his lips. "Wait. One more thing." He put up one finger. "One more thing."

Gideon led them out into the cold and over to the garage he had built when he first moved into the house. There was a metal, outdoor staircase. He leapt up the steps and showed them a large room above the garage, almost like an attic with a slanted ceiling.

He swallowed the last bit of Dorito. "I know this may seem childish, but I made us a blanket fort. It took me like two hours."

There were blankets everywhere. Blankets of all kinds and shapes and colors. They were spread out on the floor, dangling from the ceiling, and hanging on the walls. It was a colorful maze of blankets.

"I thought," Gideon added, "that it could be like when we were kids, and I would come over to your house, and we'd sleep in your music room, and we'd make blanket forts and stay up all night listening to some tunes, shining flashlights on the ceiling, and watching movies on your laptop. Remember?"

Dave looked around for a long moment, deep in thought. Finally, he said, "Giddy. This is the stupidest blanket fort I've ever seen." Then, he laughed and gave him a hug. "I love it!"

⁓

Chloe's Jeep careened down the steep, windy road until they miraculously made it down Rainmaker Mountain.

"Ok," she said. "Where is . . . they? I mean. Where are they? Where is Ariel?"

"Well, if they knew that, they wouldn't be lost."

"So then why are we driving out into the darkness to find them? We can't just drive around randomly and bump into them."

Katie was biting her nails and intently watching the glow of her phone screen. "I'm trying to figure out where they are. I asked them to drop a pin and share their location."

"Ok. I'm gonna pull over until you hear back."

"Ok."

"Stop biting your nails, girl. Ariel's gonna be just fine. We don't live in the wild wild west."

"What about coyotes? Or bears?"

"Tell them to stay in the car."

"Ok. Ok. They shared their location. They're on Sawmill Lane. Looks like near the mill."

"Well, shoot, girl. That's only like five minutes away."

"It's like ten minutes."

"Hold onto your butt!" She slammed the accelerator. Gravel kicked up and pinged around beneath the Jeep, and they took off down the road.

"Chloe!"

～

Dave was playing tackle football, concussion and all. They were in the room above Gideon's garage. Dave and Gideon against Jonah and Luke. They navigated their way through the maze of the blanket fort. Gideon, of course, tore right through, leaving a wake of trampled blankets in his path. Dave played QB, and Gideon just steamrolled everybody. Luke and Jonah didn't stand a chance, but Dave felt free and whole, not worrying about anything. Just breathing and running and throwing and letting his body do the work. His mind could rest.

At one point, he slipped on a blanket and fell hard to the hard floor. Gideon rushed over to him.

"You ok, dude?"

Dave laughed. "I feel spectacular."

～

They found Ariel's Honda Civic pulled awkwardly off the road. From where the car was parked, they could see the old mill through the trees in the dark and hear Picture Creek bubbling through the rocks.

Katie got out of the car and ran over to the Civic. She gave Ariel a hug in the moonlight as it broke into beams through the branches.

"You ok?"

"Yeah. I'm fine. I'm sorry. The last thing I wanna be is a drama queen. Sorry I took you away from your party."

"No. What? What're talking about? It couldn't possibly be a party without you, right?"

"Ariel. This is my best friend, Chloe."

Chloe was leaning on her Jeep. She gave a little wave.

"Hi," Ariel said.

"Hey. Thanks for coming. Hop on in. You can follow me to the lodge. But you're gonna have to flip on the afterburners on that Civic."

~

After the football game ended abruptly when Gideon and Luke butted heads in a nasty collision, the four guys jumped in sleeping bags and camped out in the blanket fort. Dave stared up at the dark ceiling. There were streaks of moonlight that shivered on the walls.

"What're you gonna do about Katie," Gideon asked him in the dark.

"I don't know, man. I change my mind every five minutes. I can't just, like, leave her at the altar on Saturday. That would be tragic. I can't do that to her. But I just don't know what to do."

"Well, she's doing it to herself. She can't spring this on you one week before the wedding. That's what's tragic."

"Yeah, man. We should've talked about it months ago. She should've trusted me with this months ago. I don't really understand why she didn't. Maybe it's a hard thing to talk about, but we can do hard things together."

"Or she should just check herself, bro. Seriously, she can't go changing the Gospel. That's dangerous, dude. I think you need to drop her like a bag of dirt."

"I don't know, man. It's Katie. She's the love of my life."

"Dude. She's gonna derail your life. I get this is serious stuff and crazy, messed up the way it's going down. But you gotta think about this. She's gonna bring you down and lead you astray. Think about your ministry, bro. She's gonna put you at odds with your lead pastor, like, all the time."

"I think I can handle that. And that job was always meant to be temporary. The end goal is for us to start our own ministry together. Plant a church or do missionary work or something like that."

"That's crazy, dude. How're you gonna be in ministry with her when you don't agree."

"You can have unity without uniformity."

"What're talking about? Is that a bumper sticker? You gotta be in lockstep, brother. That's the only way it's gonna work."

"I don't. . ."

"And, bro. Before you can start your own church, you have to get established. You can't establish any ministry of your own if your lead pastor doesn't trust you to control your wife."

"It's not about control, Gid."

"You have to lead," Gid told him, pressing his pointer finger into the center of Dave's chest. "God Himself gave you that responsibility. That's your cross to bear, bro. Like it or not, dude. If you go forward with this, you gotta make her toe the line."

Dave shook his head. "It's not like that. Never been like that with us. We're a team."

Gideon took his turn shaking his head. "You're lost, bro. You gotta man up and end it."

"But God brought her into my life. He's the one planted this seed in our hearts for each other."

"Feelings are fleeting. God's word is eternal."

"But what is God's word? God's words spoke the universe into existence. All of creation is God's word. His word is all around us."

"What? That's new age trash. Get that out of your head. What is wrong with you? God's word is the Bible. End of story."

"There's no end of the story, Gid. You don't think God still speaks in our lives?"

"Of course He does. Through his word. Through the Bible."

"Well, the Bible tells us to love one another like He loved us. And He doesn't stop loving us just because we change our minds or make a mistake or drift away from Him."

"No. But He'll send you to hell if you don't believe that He died for your sins and rose again."

"Will He?"

"Yes. Come on, man. This is what she's doing to you, and it's only been a week. Think about where you're gonna be thirty years from now. Think about how she's already leading you astray. Open your eyes, dude!"

Dave breathed out slowly. He looked up at the shifting moonlight on the dark ceiling. He blinked, and it felt like it took him several minutes to open his eyes again. "She believes that He died for our sins and rose again," he said finally.

"Does she?"

"I don't know." That's when a tear popped on his eyelash and streaked down his face.

"Screw this, dude. You do whatever you want. But I can't be here for you when shingles starts to go down in your marriage. You can't call me and complain about how hard it is, man. I'll be your friend. You'll always be my boy. You know I'll always love you, bro. And I would do anything for you. You need help moving, I'm there. You need me to stand up for you, I'm there. But you can't talk to me about this after today. You know where I stand."

Dave rolled over to his side. The sleeping bag swished. He closed his eyes.

~

Katie, Chloe, and Ariel had to wait again for a table at the restaurant. They found a cozy spot by the fireplace while they waited.

"So I talked to my dad the other day," Ariel said.

"Oh, wow. That's great! How did it go," Katie asked.

"Good. He hates me. No. I'm joking. But kind of. He cried. I cried. I told him I love him, and he said, 'Are you still gay?' And I told him I'm not gay, dad. I've never been gay. He just doesn't understand me, but I guess on some level I shouldn't expect him to. You know, his dad was a real strict mean old man. My dad told me stories. He used to beat my dad with a belt buckle if, like, he looked at him sideways or didn't cut the grass just the right way or whatever. And, like, I get it. That would mess me up too, so I understand on some level what he's going through, but he's gotta make some kind of effort to understand me and what I'm going through."

"He's afraid," Katie told him.

"That's exactly it. He's afraid. And I feel bad for him. You can't go through life letting yourself be directed by fear. I mean I'm afraid. I'm afraid all the time. I wake every morning, and that's the first thing I think of is something to be afraid about. Afraid someone's gonna hurt me or I'm gonna be attacked in a parking lot somewhere. I was afraid driving here even. Afraid I was gonna get lost. And then I did. But, like, I'm ok. The world keeps on turning, dad."

"It's good you were able to have a good talk with him."

"I know. And I'm grateful. I really am, but at some point it's like, when is he gonna just accept me? And listen to me and love me for who I am? I mean, isn't that what Jesus taught? Didn't Jesus teach us to love others? Even criminals and people we disagree with and people who are different than us. That was His whole thing. And my dad, this beacon of Christianity, or whatever, who hasn't missed a Sunday in, like, 30 years even that time he drove a nail through his hand and spent all night in the ER. He still got up the next morning and drove us all to church. Still in his suit and tie. How could he be so blind to the message? Why doesn't he get it?"

"I don't know. I'm sorry."

"It's ok. It's not your fault. How's the food here? Is it good?"

"Oh. It's the best. It's boujee. You'll love it."

"What should I get? Do they have anything artisanal?

"Um. I don't know. Do you know, Chloe?"

Chloe grabbed a menu from a rack on the wall and handed it to Ariel. "Let's focus on Katie," she said. She placed her hand on Katie's hand and looked her firm in the eyes. "Katie, my love. In two days, you're gonna marry the man of your dreams, the love of your life. Your best friend. And I couldn't be happier for you. I couldn't be prouder of you for your honesty. For your compassionate heart. For the love you have for everyone you meet. You are gonna be an amazing wife, and I can't wait to see you blossom." She could tell that she was about to cry. And so was Katie.

"Are you not postponing the wedding," Ariel asked.

Chloe stared daggers. A single tear slipped down her cheek. She slashed it away. "She is not."

"Ok. Sheesh. I was just asking. It's something she and I had talked about. That's all."

"But we're here at her bachelorette party, Ariel. We're not here just catching up and having a fancy dinner. We're celebrating Katie and her beautiful love story with Dave. That's why you're here."

"Ok."

Then, Chloe wrapped her arms around Katie and gave her a deep hug. "I love you, Katie. I'm so happy for you."

"Love you too, Chloe."

⁓

They were all almost asleep, just teetering on the verge of a dream, when Gideon suddenly jumped up and shouted, "I almost forgot! I can't believe I almost forgot! Get up! Get up! Guys! Get up!"

Bleary-eyed, Dave and his two brothers slowly sat up.

"Giddy, what?"

"I almost forgot the coolest part! Come this way!"

"I thought the coolest part was the sleeping part," Jonah said.

"No. This is even cooler!" Gideon led them to a door that they had all previously thought just led to a bathroom or a closet or something. He paused for a moment with his hand on the doorknob. He looked each person dead in the eyes for a flash of a second, and then he opened the door with a flourish. "Tada!"

It was a tiny room that may have previously been a small bathroom or a walk-in closet, but it was completely full of musical instruments and sound equipment.

"I call it the Rock Box," he told them. And like a little kid, he ran and jumped behind the drum kit. As always, Dave grabbed the guitar. It was a Fender Squire electric that Gideon probably got dirt cheap off of Facebook Marketplace. He loves Facebook Marketplace. He'll drive six hours to save $100.

Dave flung the strap over his shoulder. He plugged into a Marshall amp and started tweaking the settings. He knows the sound he likes. Gideon plunked a set of noise-canceling headphones on his ears. "Concussion," he said, rapping his knuckles gently on Dave's forehead. Jonah chose the bass, and Luke sat down at the keyboard.

And they jammed. Dave laid down a bluesy riff, and the band followed. Gideon was a drummer in the sense that he hit things, but holding down a tempo was never really in his wheelhouse. He typically slowed down a bit on his fills and frequently hit late on his snare, but the Ecchols brothers had jammed with him enough to know his idiosyncrasies. And the three of them had a telepathic bond that kept them automatically tight, so they each had the bandwidth to quickly adjust to Giddy's off-kilter rhythms. And Giddy liked to play fast, as fast as he possibly could, and that made jamming with him fun. He also had a really good, natural swing to his eighth notes, and the Ecchols brothers really liked playing around with that. So they had a blast, jamming.

~

When they finally got their table, they ordered right away, because they were all starving. While they were waiting for their food, the three of them were very quiet until suddenly, a random twenty-something woman with purple hair and her three friends approached their table, giggling.

"Are you thumbs up girl from that one movie," asked purple hair.

Chloe smiled at the girls and then suddenly flashed a goofy grin and a double thumbs up. The four girls all huddled around her for a selfie. And then they left giggling. "Thank you," they shouted back at her.

"What the hell was that," Ariel asked.

"Chloe was in a movie called . . . what was it called?"

"Afterglow." Chloe was nervously folding and unfolding her napkin.

"Yeah. Afterglow. A few years ago. It was her first role in Hollywood. Very small movie, but it just got picked up on Hulu, so it's gaining some slow notoriety."

"You're an actress," blurted Ariel. They batted their eyes. "Like a real actress."

Chloe grimaced and then nodded. "Yes. I am both real and an actress. Ariel, let me ask you this. Do you know Millie Bobby Brown?"

"Of course. Stranger Things. Enola Holmes. Godzilla vs. Kong. Damsel."

"Yeah. See." Chloe looked over at Katie. "Ariel knows Millie Bobby Brown."

"I'm sorry I don't know Millie Bobby Brown."

Chloe looked over at Ariel. "She doesn't even like movies." Then, she made an open-jawed expression.

Ariel laughed. "I know. It's sad, right. All she does is read."

"I mean, who does that?"

Ariel shrugged. "And she doesn't even read fun books. She reads, like, books on theology or whatever."

Chloe laughed. "What 26-year-old woman reads theology books for fun?"

"Lots of them, actually," Katie piped in.

"No. I'm pretty sure you're the only one."

They all laughed.

"But wait," Ariel said suddenly. "Do you actually know Millie Bobby Brown?"

～

Dave was stomping out the rhythm to help keep Gideon in time, and it was working. They were playing fast. It was getting hot in the Rock Box. They were all sweating.

Dave took a final solo. He wasn't thinking. He just let his fingers fly, and they fell on all the right notes. He closed his eyes, and with the sound made murky by the headphones, he felt like he was underwater. And his feet were weightless.

Suddenly, he stopped playing, and he sat down on the floor with the guitar still strung around his neck. He didn't pray in words. He didn't have the words. Didn't know the words he needed. His prayer was silent. Or maybe it wasn't. Maybe there were words he didn't know. Maybe there were sounds coming out of him and spilling on the floor. Maybe they weren't sounds. Maybe they were images. Family photos. Pictures of a house. A video of him preaching. A sonogram of a baby. Maybe they weren't images. Maybe it was just air pouring in and out of his lungs.

～

That night, they were laying in bed in their room at the lodge. Katie couldn't sleep. She was going over the playlist for tomorrow. It was only a 45-minute trip, and she had 4 hours of songs. Rich Mullins. Jars of Clay. Shane and Shane. Brandon Lake. Bethel Music. Hillsong. Songs that mattered to them. Songs they had sung together. Songs they listened to together.

She closed her eyes and said a silent prayer. It wasn't a prayer exactly. She just opened her heart to God. For a moment, she finally felt at peace. Then, she fell asleep.

Chapter 7

Friday

As promised, Katie pulled into Dave's driveway at 10:57. The clouds were dense and white and sharply angled, criss-crossing over the treetops. There were little peeks of blue behind the clouds where light streamed down in glances and lit up random pine needles, making all the trees look like they had patches of gray hair.

Katie knocked on the door, and Dave opened it quick. He looked sleepy—she noticed right away. He blinked at her in the light and rubbed his eyes.

"What's up," he told her.

"Hey."

Dave had just gotten home about twenty minutes earlier. Gideon had driven him back once he woke up. Dave hardly slept.

"How was your bachelor party," she asked him.

"Oh. Good. It was fun. The pizza was great! And I forgot how much I like Doritos."

"Doritos?"

"Yeah."

"Those're gross."

"Yeah. I guess, but somehow Gid's Root Shine made 'em taste amazing."

"That root beer was great!"

"I know. He made it in his basement."

"I know."

Dave stepped up into Katie's new pickup and settled into the rubbery bench seat. "This is nice," he told her.

"Well, it's a bag of bolts. But it's mine." She backed down the driveway. And headed out down the road.

"Where we going?"

"It's a secret," she told him with a grin.

"Ok." He smiled.

Katie cued up the music and set it to shuffle. The first song was *Worthy of it All* by Shane and Shane. A great song, but it starts a little slow. She was hoping for something more upbeat to start. So she skipped it, which was not at all how she wanted to start things off. She frowned. Dave saw it. He shifted in his seat. The next song was *Love Song for a Savior* by Jars of Clay. Also, not really what she was hoping for, but she let it play.

They drove a while in silence, feeling the ups and downs and turns in the road, watching the trees rush by, and listening to the music.

Katie turned to him and touched him on the knee. "Hey."

He looked at her.

"Do you know that line in Tozer," she said, "where he talks about the gaze of the soul meeting the gaze of God. And that's where Heaven is right here on earth?"

"Yeah."

"I love that. And I believe that's your vision as a worship pastor. God is always watching, always seeing. But when we truly turn our hearts, turn the gaze of our soul to Him, that's when we can have peace. You get that. You see that. And I think it's your calling to help people learn to truly turn the gaze of their hearts toward God. I think that's something that has gotten lost as our society has started moving faster and faster, and we've all just gotten busier and busier. And technology has stolen away our attention. You still see how important the gaze of the soul is and how it brings life and meaning. I believe in that too. I truly believe in that. I think it's an absolutely beautiful thing that you wanna do that with your ministry. I will support you in this vision. 100 percent. I will never do anything to compromise that vision for you. And I think you feel that and know that, but maybe you're starting to doubt it for some reason. Please don't doubt that. Because that is my heart too. It's my heart, because it's your heart. And our hearts are one. We still beat as one. I feel that, David. I know that in my bones. I know it deeper than I've ever known anything."

Dave nodded. His jaw was tense. His eyes hard. He didn't look at her. Finally, after a long, uncomfortable pause, he said, "I know, Katie." He looked down at his boots.

They drove in silence for a while. He tried to figure out where they were going by the roads Katie was taking, but he had no idea. He had no idea where they were. He didn't recognize anything, couldn't remember ever being on this road in his whole life, even though they were only about twenty minutes away from home.

Finally, after a long, sad silence, he asked her, "What do you think about abortion?"

She looked over at him, her mouth slightly open. "What?"

"Abortion. Where do you stand?"

"Why does that matter?"

"It matters, Katie. You know how important this issue is to me. And to my family. You know the story of my Aunt Sarah. It's important to me."

She swallowed. "Well . . ." She waited. She adjusted her grip on the steering wheel. Her fingers were sticky. She swallowed again. "I don't think it's a black and white issue."

"It is, Katie. It's completely black and white."

"You can only say that, because you've never faced a situation where you've had to make that decision."

"Yes. Because I've made the right decisions in my life so I'd never be in that situation. People end up in that situation because they've made wrong decisions."

"Have you ever made a wrong decision?"

"Of course."

"Well, what if that one decision changed the course of your whole life? And took away all the opportunities you have? And just turned your life upside down?"

"That's garbage, Katie. I make the right decisions on things with lasting consequences. Or at least I don't make catastrophic decisions. And if I did, I would stand up and take responsibility. I would accept the consequences. I wouldn't turn my back on them."

"Would you?"

"Yes. I would never kill a baby just to make my life a little easier."

"David. That's ridiculous. You're making it sound like it's evil."

"It is evil."

"But what if it's not even a bad decision? What about the case of rape?"

"Katie. You know the statistics as well as I do. You know that less than one percent of abortions are done because of rape. Thirty percent of abortions are done by young, single women who just don't want to be bothered to have a baby."

"You can't possibly know that."

"That's the statistics."

"I don't think that's true, but that's not the heart of the issue. What's at the center is that you think you should be able to make that choice for everyone even though you've never walked a mile in their shoes."

"It isn't a choice, Katie. It's murder!"

"That's an extremely black and white way of framing it."

"Because it is black and white."

"Your Aunt Sarah."

"Yeah?"

"She was 19. 19! She made a mistake. That mistake shouldn't derail her whole life. She was in college. She had no job. No money. What choice did she really have?"

"Aunt Sarah would tell you even today, that she should've made a different decision. She tells people that all the time."

"Yeah. That's what she says now. But back then, when she was in the middle of it, her life was different. Her whole life shouldn't be judged by it's worst moment."

"Of course not. I'm not judging her. She realizes what she did was wrong. And it breaks her heart. I'm not judging her."

"Would you judge her if she stood by that decision after all these years?"

"I don't know. Probably. Because God is convicting her heart, and she would be turning from it."

"It's not right to judge someone for a making a decision in the midst of a horrific situation that you've never even come close to experiencing anything like it."

"It's not about judging anyone!" His voice was rising. "It's about saving the life of a baby. Aunt Sarah thinks about that baby all the time. It haunts her. That baby would be what? Almost 30 now? She never got a chance to live. Never took a breath or saw a tree or tasted pizza. Never knew love. Only cruelty. Oh my god, Katie. You're awful. Just awful. How could you even. . ." He was crying. "It's disgusting." He shook his head.

"I'm not awful just because I disagree with you."

"But you know how I feel on this issue, Katie."

"Then why on earth did you ask me about it? Are you just trying to pick a fight with me? I'm trying to bring us together here. I'm trying to focus on the things that bind us together. Not the things that could tear us apart. And what are you doing? You're focusing on the things that're gonna tear us apart. Why?"

"What happened to 'you created my inmost being. You knit me together in my mother's womb?' Katie, we're fearfully and wonderfully made. This is insanity. We can't go on like this! How can we go on like this? Why should we pretend this is gonna work?"

"We're not pretending," she shouted. She was crying now too. "Who's pretending? We love each other. We're meant for each other. This is love. It's not always pretty. Sometimes it's hard. But that doesn't mean it's not worth it."

"Love is patient. Love is kind. It is not self-seeking."

"Are you saying I'm self-seeking? Or I'm not kind."

"Are we being kind to each other right now? Is this love?"

"Sometimes love is ugly and hurtful. But it keeps no record of wrongs. And where does it say love is always in agreement? We can work this out if we have love for each other. We can conquer anything if we have love."

"I don't know, Katie."

"It was Tozer. He said, 'You can see God from anywhere if your mind is set to love and obey Him.' So as long as we have love for God and love for each other, then we are always in His presence. No matter what."

"Tozer also said, 'One hundred pianos all tuned to the same fork are automatically tuned to each other.' Right now, we're not tuned to the same fork. You're abandoning Scripture, Katie. You're twisting it, because you wanna be hip and cool, and you wanna fit in with your new friends at your secular school."

"That's not fair. I'm just as rooted now in Scripture as I've ever been. My friends at college made fun of me constantly for being a Christian, for reading the Bible. You don't know what you're talking about."

"Maybe you're not abandoning it, but you're twisting it."

"I'm not twisting it. I just disagree with some of your interpretations. That doesn't make me wrong. Doesn't make you wrong either."

"You're too casual about sinful things. Sin is real and damaging. And it will destroy you from the inside out. The Bible tells us over and over to resist temptation. And you're, like, de-emphasizing the negative impact of sin in someone's lives. It's not nothing. Even though, we're forgiven, sin still damages your soul."

"I don't disagree with that, but I think you're too rigid. And there's no one sin that is more damaging than any others. And we all sin."

"And your negativity toward the church is also tearing me apart, because it . . ."

"Tearing you apart?"

"Well, it's conflicting, because we decided together that we were going into full-time ministry within the church. And I don't even understand your critique of THE CHURCH. Because every single church is different. You're never gonna find the perfect church, because it's made up of flawed people. But you find a church where you can serve."

"Well God forbid you ever be conflicted, David. We have always challenged each other. It's good for us to grow together. And also, Tozer critiqued THE CHURCH. Didn't he say something like, 'The church is famishing for want of God's presence?'"

"But our God is not a God of confusion."

"But of peace."

"Yes."

"But the world is full of confusion."

"Yes."

"So it doesn't say that you're never gonna be confused. But God can bring you peace even in the midst of confusion."

Dave finally looked up and realized that it was snowing. Big, fluffy flakes so thick it looked like a wool blanket.

"It's snowing," he said.

"Yeah."

"I just noticed. How long has it been like this?"

"A while."

"Where are we going?" He peered through the falling snow and caught a flash of recognition. "Are we in Mahaffey?"

"Yes."

"Are we going to Mahaffey Camp?"

"Yes."

"Why?"

"Because Tozer."

"What about Tozer?"

"He used to speak here all the time."

"Really?"

"Yeah. Like every year. He actually grew up just a few miles from the camp."

They were on Route 219, which was covered with snow. All the trees were frosted white. A white mountain emerged slowly on the horizon, and the sky was white. Everything was white. The whiteness was so thick there was almost no sunlight. But what little light there was bounced all around and left a gloomy white glow like everything was haunted by the ghost of itself.

As the white mountain in the distance grew larger, the Mahaffey Camp sign began materializing into view, draped in white. When they got close enough, they could see that the sign said, "Have a Merry Christmas!"

Past the sign, there were two stone pillars at the entrance, and Katie eased the car between them and onto Kings Highway, which circled the camp. She turned left at the camp office and parked in a small lot beneath a tall, thin tree flanked by two shorter ones, and it reminded her of Jesus on the cross with the two thieves. The thought of it stopped her for a second before she shut off the engine.

"What're we doing here," Dave snapped.

"We're gonna walk around and worship. We're gonna find God in this place. We're gonna tune our pianos to the same fork." And then, she stopped before stepping down out of the truck. She looked over at him and said, 'Rise up my love, my fair one, and come away.'"

They both stepped down out of the truck. Snow dissolved in their hair. They were both struck by the eerie silence. There was no sound but the wind. In the distance, they saw the bright green roof of the Main Tabernacle as it was slowly hidden by the falling snow.

Dave buttoned his coat and pulled his gloves from his pocket to put them on. He ran a few steps to catch up to Katie. His boots crunched in the snow. When he caught up to her, he could hear her breathing.

"You cold," he asked.

"I'm good. You?"

"Little bit."

She smiled at him. He blinked. They walked past a rock that said, "God is able to do immeasurably more than we ask or imagine."

They made their way toward the Main Tabernacle. Dave had a song in his head. He couldn't quite place it, but somehow, it caught the mood perfectly.

In front of the Tabernacle, there was another rock that said, "With God all things are possible."

"All things are possible," she said, almost under her breath.

Dave looked up at the churning sky and the shimmering glow of snow. He wasn't sure he believed it. Wasn't sure he ever believed it. All things simply aren't possible. A triangle can't have four sides. Two plus two can't equal five. A camel can't pass through the eye of a needle. A person can't jump over the Lincoln Monument. What did the Apostle Paul even mean when he said that? But maybe somehow Katie actually does believe it. Maybe that's why she thinks this could possibly work, that they could actually have a happy marriage. Because with God all things are possible.

Dave remembered reading a book a long time ago. *Experiencing God* by Henry Blackaby. It was about just fully trusting God with everything. Trusting Him without evidence or without a plan or without any clear idea of what the future holds. Just diving headlong into whatever you believe God is calling you to do. Dave wasn't like that. Was never like that. He had to have a plan. He had to think it out. He had seen his friends dive into crazy situations, because they believed God had been calling them into it. His friend Aaron, who he had grown up with in youth group, had jumped into the mission field right out of college. He served over in China for not quite a year when he ran out of funding and had to return, and he ended up with enormous debt that he's going to be paying off for over a decade. And he would just talk about what a great experience it was and how he had no regrets. And God taught him so much and is still teaching him responsibility and discipline. But now, he and his fiancée and planning a wedding, and he's going to begin their marriage by saddling her with his debt. None of that was right. Dave knew that wasn't of God. That was a failure. How could a failed missions trip that leaves you and your family completely broke for a decade be part of God's plan? Dave couldn't wrap his head around it.

But Dave knew that Katie was different from him in that way. She followed her heart. Did that mean that she was more Spirit-led than he was? Or did it just mean that she was more prone to making bad choices? In the past, Dave had always looked at it like they balanced each other out. He was the head. She was the heart. She could trust that all things are possible. He would keep them grounded.

But maybe it wouldn't be like that at all. Maybe she would drag him into bad decisions that would take their whole family off course.

"This is probably where he would've spoke," Katie said, looking up at the Main Tabernacle.

"Who?"

"Tozer," she replied, shifting her eyes at him.

"Do you think it would have been in this same building?"

"I don't know."

"That would have been, what? The 40's?"

"I think so." She pulled out her cell phone. "They have a history up on their website." She started punching buttons on her phone. "Oh," she said. "No service here."

"Do you think he talked about the things that he wrote about in his books?"

"Probably. Do you remember when we came here for youth camp?"

He smiled. "I do."

"You brought your guitar, and you played and sang all day long."

"And you sat right beside me the whole time, singing harmony."

She nodded. "I did. There wasn't any other place I'd rather be."

Dave took in that last sentence like a breath. He felt it to be true. Then and still true now. And it was a beautiful thing to have someone trust you and love you in that way. But there was also a weight to it. And it somehow took him by surprise. The responsibility of being loved.

The snow crunched under his boot as he turned and started walking through the snow toward the bridge.

Katie sensed Dave walk away, but she kept looking up at the Tabernacle, watching the wind blow the snow off the roof in cursive loops. She could see the icicles shining on the eaves. She could feel the Spirit like a soft wind glancing through her hair and across her cheeks.

Finally, she closed her eyes and turned to follow him over the bridge. She was starting to shiver. The snow was falling in hectic ribbons. It was like they were inside a snow globe that was being shook. She ran to catch up with him at the end of the bridge.

He turned to her and said, "Maybe we should head back. It's really starting to come down."

"Can we go just a little further?"

"Ok."

On the far side of the bridge, they walked past a stone campfire ring with burnt shards of wood and ash. Around the fire ring were makeshift seats made out of stumps or stones and a few wooden benches. She remembers gathering there one night long ago with the youth group, singing worship songs and roasting marshmallows.

Through the blinding snow, they walked on. Katie wondered if their life was a movie, what song would be playing over this scene. Would it be a sad song? Would it be hopeful? Would it build slowly and swell with emotion? Would it be simple and quiet and contemplative?

Had she done enough to save their relationship? Did their relationship even need saving? She wasn't sure. Honestly, she had no idea. She could feel the tension building in the song in her heart. It was a minor key. The chords were dissonant and sad and full of longing. The melody was clear and beautiful but uncertain of itself, so it wandered.

Finally, they came upon a final scripture rock. This one said, "And now these three remain: faith, hope, and love, but the greatest of these is love."

The snow was so thick, it was difficult to see. It was a white blanket over the world. Dave put his arm gently around her shoulders.

"Let's go," he told her. And he guided her back in the direction of the truck. He kept his arm around her, and they walked together, their feet sliding into rhythm with each other. Looking down, they navigated by following their own footprints in reverse. By the time they came to the Tabernacle, their footprints were gone, covered over with snow.

Dave could feel her shoulders going up and down as she breathed, and he knew that she was relying completely on him. Or maybe she was trusting God, but she was relying on him as God's angel to get her back to the truck and out of the snow.

When he looked around, he saw nothing but white. But then he looked up and saw a green flash of the Tabernacle roof. He remembered which direction they had come to the Tabernacle, so he turned in that general direction and started walking, his arm still around her. They walked together pushing into the wind. They could feel snowflakes stinging their faces as the wind whistled and crashed around them. The wind blew hard. He could feel Katie's body shivering. He could see the silhouette of some trees, but everything blurred with snow.

He said a prayer to God. The words weren't as important as the simple act of turning the gaze of his soul from his circumstances toward God. And his inward gaze met the gaze of God looking back at him, and in that moment, he felt a wave of calm. He knew they weren't going to die out there at Mahaffey Camp and their bodies frozen in ice only to be excavated a thousand years later and all the scientists marveling at this ancient couple frozen together arm in arm. Would the scientists make up stories about them? Would they be called the lovers of Mahaffey? The gaze of God was a pick-axe to his soul that cracked the ice and let the water bubble up and flow, and the cracks stretched like a child's waking fingers throughout his whole body and mind and spirit. And he knew they were just two specks of dust floating in the vastness of space and time. But he knew also that God was right now counting the hairs on their heads. And it was all true at once.

When he looked up, he saw the blur of the three crosses in the gloom glow of snow, and the tallest one in the middle was Jesus. He knew the truck was nearby. He picked her up into his arms and carried her the rest of the way to the truck. The door hinges groaned. He set her in the driver's seat, and she shivered. He got in on the passenger side. He dug through her pockets to find the keys. Then, he turned on the truck and cranked up the heater. Within a few minutes, the windows fogged over and their bodies began to thaw.

"I can't believe how fast," Katie said. "That went bad. So fast." Her body was still recovering. Her mind too. She looked down at her fingers in amazement. They felt like electricity pulsed in them.

"I think we should wait here until the snow lets up," he told her.

"No." Slowly, she sat up straight. "Our rehearsal."

"Well, that's still almost four hours away."

"But it could take us two hours to get home in this snow."

"Maybe. But once it lets up, we'll be home in an hour."

"What if it doesn't let up."

"It's gonna let up."

"How do you know?"

He pulled out his cell phone to check the weather forecast. "No service," he told her. "It's just too dangerous to drive in this right now."

"Ok."

So they waited. They waited in silence for nearly a full hour. The snow was still coming down pretty good, but it did let up some, so they decided to start driving. Katie drove very slowly and carefully. After a few miles, they saw a car. A beat up, old Chevy Cavalier. It looked like it had spun out into a snowbank about 15 feet from the road. It was obviously stuck.

"We have to stop and help," Katie said.

"No. I think we should just go. I'm sure they have a cell phone and have already called somebody."

"There's no service out here. They need help."

He shrugged.

Katie steered the truck slowly to the side of the road. While she was hitting the brake, the truck skidded on a patch of ice and went a little further off the road than expected, but it came to a stop without any problems. They both got out of the truck and walked down to the beat-up Chevy. As they got closer, they could see the silhouette of a young child in a car seat through the back seat window. A young woman got out of the car.

"Hi," she told them.

"Hello. Do you need some help?"

"Yes. Oh my god. I can't believe you stopped. We've been stuck here, like, an hour, and you're the first car we saw this whole time. Do you have any cell phone reception? I can't get a signal."

Dave and Katie both tried their phones again, but they were still in a dead spot. "No service. What happened?"

"I don't know," the woman said. "It all happened so fast. We just hit an ice patch, and the car slid and then started spinning. Before we knew it, we were way over here."

"What's your name," Katie asked.

"I'm Cassie. That's my son, Chase." She motioned toward the backseat of the car.

Dave and Katie both smiled and waved at Chase. He looked back at them from behind the glass.

Cassie had a cardboard box in her trunk. Dave used it to dig out the snow from around her rear wheels. It was slow going with a cardboard box and the snow still falling. After about 15 minutes, he had mostly dug the car out of the snowbank. Next, he started making a clear path for the car up to the road. While he was doing that, Katie noticed that one of Cassie's rear tires was flat. Dave hadn't noticed. He was in too big of a hurry to get Cassie on her way and out of their lives.

Katie went around behind the car, but before she could get the trunk open, she noticed some white, stenciled letters on the rear window, "RIP Johnny. 1997–2022. Loving Husband and Father."

Katie opened the Cavalier's trunk and lifted up the base of it to find the hidden compartment underneath. There, she found a spare tire and a lug wrench. She went to work. But the lug nuts were too tight. She couldn't budge them. She tried over and over as hard as she could. The palms of her hands were going numb before she finally stopped. And she sat down in the snow and started crying. She was crying for the futility of life and the fall of humankind. She cried hard for several minutes. Then, suddenly, her eyes brightened. And she stopped crying. With her gloves, she wiped the tears from her cheeks. There is hope in serving others, she told herself. There is hope in serving others. "Bear one another's burdens," she said quietly to herself. "And fulfill the law of Christ." And she fought with the lug wrench. She wrestled against it like Jacob in the desert. She gritted her teeth, and she fought. With all her heart and with all her mind and with all her strength.

Dave stopped as he came around the Cavalier. He had finished clearing a path and was coming back to throw the box in the trunk. But then he saw Katie on her knees in the snow. And something about the sight of her tied his heart in a knot. He still loved her. He didn't breathe for several seconds.

He watched her struggle. He knew she would be a good wife. He knew she would be a great mother to their kids. "Bear one another's burdens."

Finally, he stepped forward to help her. He touched her lightly on the shoulder. "I got it," he told her. She stopped suddenly as if coming out of a dream. Her hair fell in front of her face. She handed him the lug wrench and moved out of the way. He took on the responsibility of wrestling against the wheel. Now, it was his fight too. And he fought. It wouldn't budge. It was stuck. He put all his weight on it. It didn't move. Then, he got up and stood on the wrench, with his hand on the roof of the car to steady himself. And then he jumped and landed on the thin metal bar with all his weight. He did it again. Katie came over and started pulling up on the other end of the wrench. She pulled up, and he jumped down on the other side. Until. It turned. When the wrench turned, he fell. Katie tried to catch him, but they both crashed together into the snow.

Cassie started the car and cranked the accelerator. Dave and Katie pushed from behind. The wheels spun, kicking up gray snow onto Katie's pantlegs. Their lungs breathed in cold air and exhaust. Their hearts pounded. The wheels spun and spun. The back end of the car slipped side to side. Snow flung in all directions. Dave's boot lost traction, and he fell to one knee. But he got right back up, knowing that if the car slipped back down the ice, it could crush both of them.

Finally, the wheels took hold, and the Cavalier bolted up to the road. Dave and Katie fell into the snow, exhausted. Cassie got out of the car and came over to give them both hugs. Then, she left, and they watched her taillights disappear into the storm. Dave and Katie were both soaked with snow, and the snow was still falling. They were shivering and exhausted.

Wearily, they climbed into Katie's truck. Dave looked at the time on his phone. They still had almost two hours before their wedding rehearsal.

"We might still make it," he told her.

She nodded and started the truck. The wheels spun for a second and then they got going down the road. But something was wrong. The truck was pulling hard to the right, and they both heard a grinding noise coming from underneath the truck.

Katie pulled off the road and stopped. Dave got out to look, but she stayed in the car. A minute later, the door groaned open and he fell into the bench seat. He closed the door.

"We have a flat tire," he told her.

She started crying.

"Do you have a spare?"

"No."

~

It was four in the morning when Katie finally dropped Dave off at his house. She didn't pull into his driveway, because the snow was almost a foot high. The road had at least been plowed. He jumped down out of the truck without looking back at her. He slammed the door. It shook the truck. She watched him through the car door window. He had to lift his knees to his chest to trudge through the snow.

She drove home and just parked her car on the road. She moved without thinking up the driveway and up the porch steps. She fumbled for her keys and unlocked the door.

Chloe rushed at her and hugged her in the doorway. Their bodies slashed together in a weary embrace. After a moment, Katie collapsed into Chloe's arms. Chloe held her up.

"We thought you were dead," Chloe whispered.

"I think we're done," she said. "I think it's over."

Chapter 8

Wedding Day?

KATIE WOKE UP AT 10:30. The wedding was at 1:00.

"Get up!"

Katie groaned and rolled away like a child.

"Get up Get up Get up!"

"What are you doing, Chloe?"

"Katie, get up!"

"Why?"

"It's your wedding day! Let's go!"

"He's not coming."

"Yes he is." Chloe ripped the blankets off, and the cold hit Katie all at once.

"No. He's not, Chloe. It's over. I need sleep." She grabbed for the blankets with one eye open.

Chloe stopped her by putting her arm around her. "Katie. I love you. You're my best friend on this whole god-forsaken planet. But you have to get up now and get dressed. Because if he does show up, you need to be there, right? You don't wanna be the one not showing up. That is not what you want. I know it. You are gonna be the one that shows up for him. That shows up for your marriage. That is what you want. I know that about you. I know that is what you want. You're just hurt. And you feel defeated. But . . . isn't there a saying? Like. If it's not good, then God's not done. Well. God's not done yet with you and Dave."

Chloe bent down and grabbed Katie at the waist. Then, she lifted her up onto her shoulder.

"Put me down!"

Chloe sat her down with her feet on the floorboards. "Go take a shower. You smell like a car engine."

Katie took a long, hot shower. She came out wearing sweats.

"Let's go," Chloe told her. They went outside and trudged through the snow. The sun was shining. The light bounded off the snow and made a bright, warm bubble of light all around them.

"Did you shovel our entire driveway," Katie asked. "And did you move my truck?"

"Shut up. Get in the Jeep."

They got in, and the Jeep squealed down the road, kicking up snow and slush. When they got to the church, it was busy. There were cars and people . . . as if a wedding was going to happen later that day. Katie saw her dad in the parking lot, carrying a tray of cookies. She had to block the sun with her hand when she got out of the Jeep.

"He's not coming," she said to no one. Then she turned to Chloe and said, "Why don't they know he's not coming?"

Chloe looked straight ahead and started walking into the church. Katie followed. They went inside and down the steps to a classroom in the basement of the church—one of the classrooms where she and Dave had Sunday School when they were kids.

Letty and Liz were there already, both dressed in sweats. They were both sitting in metal folding chairs. Letty was wearing a walking boot. Her leg was stretched out long in front of her. She had crutches leaning against the wall. Both sisters lit up when Katie entered the room.

"Katie! I can't believe it! Today is the day," Liz said, jumping up and rushing over to give Katie a hug. "I'm so happy for you!"

Katie had known Liz and Letty Mackey since she was ten. Their grandparents owned a horse farm that sort of surrounded the parsonage where Katie lived. The twins used to come and stay at the farm for a month or so every summer. One day, they rode their horses over to Katie's house and gave her a ride all over the farm. Katie got to see and explore so many amazing and majestic settings that she never knew existed even though they were just a few hundred yards from her house. One time, they were riding way up on the ridge and they came into a clearing where Katie looked down and saw her own house way down below. It looked tiny, and Katie couldn't believe the sight of it.

When Katie was 12 and the twins were 14, they came to live with their grandparents, and they went to Katie's school, which was so small that K-12 was all housed in one building. They typically graduate about 40 or so students a year.

"I need a hug too," Letty said, as she got up and hobbled over.

Katie wrapped her arms around Letty's shoulders. "I heard you broke your foot."

"Yeah. Candy Cane stepped on it."

"Oh. I'm sorry."

"No. I'm sorry. I'm gonna be limping down the aisle at your wedding."

"Oh. That's ok."

Just then, Mrs. Scobee walked in the room. "Hello, my beloveds," she announced. "Katie, my darling. Congratulations! You look divine."

Katie smiled at her. Mrs. Scobee was a local artist who had been attending Katie's church for over a decade. She volunteered to do the hair and make-up for Katie and her bridesmaids. For the next hour and a half, they talked and laughed and listened to music while Mrs. Scobee fixed up their hair.

Ariel joined them about halfway through. They were dressed in a smart, black suit with a bright pink shirt. Their hair was done up in braids.

After Mrs. Scobee left, the girls got into their dresses. It was all happening. It started to feel real for Katie as she was putting on her wedding dress. As she was dressing, her mom came in. She was crying. She gave Katie a hug and handed her a gift. Katie unwrapped a shoe box. Inside was a spectacular pair of white, slingback Prada pumps.

"They're your something new," she told her.

"Thank you!" Katie was crying. "How did you afford this?"

Her mom shrugged. "I've been selling knitted socks and scarves on Pinterest for a few years."

"I didn't even know you knew how to use the internet," Katie laughed.

"Your dad helps me." She hugged Katie a second time and then left. Katie finished pulling on the dress and then tried on the new shoes. They fit perfectly.

Chloe handed her a slender, black box.

"What's this?"

"Something blue. Open it." She smiled.

Katie opened the box, and all the light in the room reflected up into her eyes and made her whole face shine. She pulled a delicate necklace with a sapphire teardrop pendant. The sapphire was encased within a silver celtic knot.

"It's beautiful! Thank you." Chloe helped her put it on.

When they were all dressed, Maggie came in and gave hugs all around. "You look beautiful," she told Katie.

"Thank you."

"I have something for you." Out of the pocket of her dress, she pulled an elegant, sterling silver cable bracelet. "My dad made this for my mom. When the Howling Run school first opened, like, sixty years ago, he took a some silversmithing classes and ended up making this."

"It's amazing," Katie said. "Oh my gosh! Thank you!" She gave out yet another hug. Everyone was smiling, beaming. When Maggie left, the girls all looked at each other and smiled. Then, Katie's eyes glassed over and she started to sob. The girls rushed around her.

"He's not coming," she said.

"Who's not coming?"

"David's not coming."

"Of course he's coming," Liz told her. "He'll be here sweetheart. Of coursehe's coming." She looked at her watch. "He's probably already here. It's only twenty minutes until the wedding."

Katie gasped for breath. She fell down into a couch in the corner of the room. "I don't think he is. I think it's over. I don't think he wants me anymore. It's . . . my . . . fault."

"Katie. No. Oh my gosh. It's gonna be ok. He's gonna be here. He loves you."

"Try calling him," Chloe told her.

Katie called him, but there was no answer. Then, Chloe called him. No answer. She texted him, "You better show up today for your wife or I will haunt you for the rest of your life."

Chloe stood up. Her face was iron. She kicked off her shoes and ran out door. She leaped up the stairs to the foyer of the church. There were people everywhere. She negotiated her way quickly through the crowd, bumping into people and sliding her body against them as she pushed her way into the sanctuary.

She saw Katie's dad up front and Katie's mom. Then, she noticed Gideon off to the side. He was dressed in his tuxedo. He was trying to put on his boutonniere. She ran over to him and caught him completely by surprise. He dropped the flowers on the floor and several petals popped off and drifted slowly in the air.

Chloe picked up the boutonniere in a flash and fastened it to his lapel. "How did you . . ."

"Where's David?"

"Haven't seen him," he snapped

"What do you mean you haven't seen him?"

"Not since yesterday morning when I dropped him off at his house."

"You're the best man. You have one job. You get him to the wedding on time. That's your job."

He held up two fingers. "I have two jobs." He reached into his pocket and pulled out the rings.

"Ok. You have two jobs. But if you don't get him here, then the rings don't matter."

"Well," his face twisted a little. "That's true, I guess."

She grabbed him by the lapels. Her eyes stabbed him in the throat, and he swallowed a thick, hard nothing. "Is he coming," she said clearly and slowly and with all the seriousness and hope in the world.

He shrugged. "I don't know."

Chloe pushed him away. She looked down at his shiny black shoes.

"She shouldn't have waited so long to tell him," he said.

She looked up at him with the saddest eyes he had ever seen. "Your Root Shine is phenomenally good," she told him.

"Thank you," he smiled.

She turned and walked away, her shoulders sagging.

Back in the bridal room, Katie was trying to call him again. When Chloe walked in, Katie jumped up. "Did you see him?"

Chloe shook her head. "He's not here."

Katie fell on the floor. She became a wedding dress puddle again. She didn't pass out exactly. Her legs just gave out. It was like they disappeared from her body just for a second and then came back. But once she was on the floor, she saw no need or reason to get up, so she stayed there. For several minutes. Nobody really knew what to do. They all just stood in shocked silence.

~

"Fear is not my future."

Katie lifted her head at the sound.

"You are."

It was Dave's voice echoing down the hallways of the church, singing one of the songs from her playlist. She blinked.

"Heartbreak's not my home. You are."

She jumped to her feet. Her ankle buckled for a moment as she steadied herself on her heels.

"Let him turn it in your favor," Dave sang from down the hallway. "Watch Him work it for your good. He's not done with what He's started. He's not done until it's good."

"Hello, peace," she sang back to him. "Hello, joy. Hello, love."

"See you out there, Squirrelbutt."

"I love you, poopyface."

Chloe appeared beside her and handed her the bouquet. "Let's go," she smiled. "He's waiting for you."

The girls ran up the stairs. The music started. Letty hobbled down the aisle. Then Liz. Then Chloe.

Then everybody stood up. Katie came around the corner. And he was standing there in the front of the sanctuary, in his tuxedo, smiling at her like he had never smiled at her before. A new smile for a new day that would be the first day in the rest of their life together.